GIANCARLO DIAGO CEVALLOS

Envoys

First edition

ISBN: 9781088264447

Cover art by Daniela Valerio

This book was professionally typeset on Reedsy. Find out more at reedsy.com

To my grandmother Maruja,
To Giada, mom, dad, and all my family.
To the world and the wind and the stars for being beautiful,
To Scout, Dixie, Scooby, Koby and Oliver;
I love all of you
*

A mi abuela Maruja,
A Giada, mama, papa, y toda mi familia,
Al mundo y el viento y las estrellas por ser bella,
A Scout, Dixie, Scooby, Koby, y Oliver
Los amo a todos

Contents

1

A Singed Hat

Once, on the cold icy shore, Taran as a child had sat for an hour just looking north. Straining his eyes. When asked why he did that, Taran explained to his mother that he wanted to see the Island. She had laughed, then apologized, and explained that the Island at the top of the world rested much too far away to see, even though the Ring was the closest landmass to it.

Taran had accepted that, but over passed time he missed the opportunity to make the long maritime pilgrimage north. Life had busied him, was all. And the chance had seemed lost forever when the Island had isolated itself. So Taran had received the news, as an adult, that the Island wanted nothing more to do with the world whose north pole it rested on.

So Taran had lived his life among his tribe, the Skulks. These rugged and hide-clad people lived on the Ring, either fighting or befriending other tribes.

For its part, the Ring was a circular landmass surrounding the Island. The coast was such a perfect curve, many assumed it to be carved, as if by some massive beast.

So Taran had lived. Sometimes in danger, often in happiness, always aging. As an old man, he was next in line to be chief, and had a large family.

Every Skulkian agreed Taran had been well blessed.

So it was that the rest of his life seemed set.

Taran had just one regret, that the Island had never opened again, and that no one ever knew why. Some brave Ring explorers had tried to reach it, just to be turned back by its human and inhuman inhabitants.

But then, strange light-skinned men came on galleons from far south. Envoys of the Astrian empire, they'd explained themselves to be. Their high-masted ships brought foreign language, foreign knowledge, and alien diseases.

As the Skulks began to grieve for their epidemic and diseased, the Astrians had already moved on, seeing nothing of worth in the Ring, and looking north.

Taran, even through his sadness at the loss of loved ones, felt a swelling in him. Was it joy? Excitement?! Not at becoming the chief, after the bed-ridden death of the last one.

But because after all these endless years, Taran would no longer be the gazer on a cold icy shore.

He would accompany Astria north and reach the Island.

* * *

The *Saint*, skipping across the waves, was one of the best of Astria's fleet. Streaks of black and green and blue painted the sails and decks and hull. Two entwined anguilla eel statues rested on the bowsprit. Astria did not have a lot it could be proud of, but of this it was. Every Astrian knew how to swim before they could walk. And the pride of the sailors almost banished their homesickness.

Taran wondered sometimes if he stood out on deck. Among spiffy sailors, who spoke a language Taran had just recently learned, he wore furs and leathers. Still, Taran kept them on. His necklace always stayed on. The faded leather cord held two charms. A faded but sharp canine tooth the size of a pinky, and a small carving of two folded hands, fashioned from obsidian.

Still, as the ship made great progress north, faster than Taran had ever imagined the journey could be done. Within two days it could be reached. The Saint could reach the Island by nightfall. As they neared the north pole, everyone needed to wear thinner clothes, the climate warmed as they reached the Island.

Elsewhere on the ship, snuggled between scrolls and paper, Captain Radial had a dilemma.

By then, Taran had learned how to speak Astrian while a few explorers had learned the Skulk language, but Radial still had plenty of problems going over translated reports and descriptions he'd stored in his cabin. When he stomped upstairs to confront Taran over them, the yellow feathers adorning Radial's sweeping blue hat bounced above deck.

Radial found Taran looking out over the ocean with a nervous smile on his face. In response, Radial tried a smile too.

"Taran, all these descriptions from you," which had been transcribed by Lunate, an explorer waiting for news on the Ring, "How am I supposed to believe these..." the Captain checked for the right term, hoping he got it right, "...beasts exist?"

Taran turned around, amused. "I thought you were an experienced sea Captain. Don't you have impressive animals and monsters in the rest of the world, too?"

"Well yes, but..." Over the course of his life, the captain

had heard many tales of demons and monsters. One of his favorite tales came from a far off-land below the equator, of a demon with massive tusks and gray feet that could flatten men whole. They called it... an elephant. But the descriptions offered by Taran were so fantastical as to be mind-boggling. Not unbelievable, as Radial knew the world was quite the big place with many mysteries, but because Radial's crew would have no way to fight off such beasts if they threatened the ship.

"Take the rammer." said Radial. "The form of a massive goat, but its charges tear down everything in front of it like massive gusts of wind. What happens if our crew meets one?"

"Be nice to it and leave it be."

"But... Eh." The captain did not like these tales, because these monsters seemed so strong as to not fit into his fantasies of trophies and fame back home. And besides, none of his crew possessed divine powers like his Emperor back home did. He switched to a different tactic. "Have you ever seen a beast? Do none wander so close to the Ring?"

"No." Taran didn't elaborate, since it was a mystery even he didn't quite know the answer to. Every tribe on the Ring held different myths to explain why animals that might as well be gods in their power only stayed around the Island and never strayed close to the Ring.

This conversation between the two continued for a while, sometimes touching on the Island's surreal geography. But there were other explorers besides the crew near the ship, and these non-human explorers were tapping and poking at the hull from under the dark underwater currents.

These young and bold adventurers were stormers. Though much different, they appeared a lot like eels, but lightning crackled under their skin and in their eyes. As kids, the three

4

were much smaller than adults, but still as thick as a barrel and longer than an anaconda. The kids poked at the hull of this strange craft. Though they were careful at first, soon they headbutted it, cheering each other on.

You, smart reader, might think all this poking would be hard with the speed the ship traveled at. How could they play with the ship if it sailed past them? Do not fret over that, the kids were fast enough to match the fifty kilometers per hour speed of the *Saint Carpal*. Whenever one stormer started wrestling or nibbling with another, they caught up again soon with a burst of wind.

Yes, wind underwater. Not a current. Such is the nature of the beasts.

While the Captain and Skulk leader squabbled on the ship about whether they'd see any beasts and what they'd do in such an event, many other beasts other than the Stormers observed the vessel from afar. Shadowy eyes and bulks in the depths of the ocean, bright eyes flapping among the fluffy clouds.

But as intelligent creatures, they stayed back and waited to see what, if any thing the *Saint Carpal* might do. The young stormers, ignorant and innocent, were the closest. Below the hull, they chatted among themselves until the largest kid made a dare and set out to confront the *Saint Carpal*, then report back to cries of adoration.

* * *

The conversation between Taran and Radial drifted away. Not

because of a lack of things to discuss. After all, Radial only knew a fraction of the stories that Taran could tell about the Island and Ring. But Taran saw the Captain's interest waning, swept away by the sea spit. Unlike his subordinate, Lunate, the Captain had little interest in legends and intrigue. Taran might've missed what drove the Captain, but Taran was old. He'd seen the greedy glint in other's eyes enough times.

"Do we disappoint you?" he asked.

It took a second for the question to pull Radial's attention away from the glittering sea and his dreams. "The Skulks, you mean? Or the land?"

"You love glory. Not adventure or mysteries—glory." Radial didn't interrupt. No need to acknowledge what they both knew. "You arrived with great expectations just to find frigid tundras with little to trade or give you, unless you want frost or pelts. And now there's a second chance for fame beyond the sea."

The Captain's hat dimmed the light across his face, casting a shadow as he leaned against the rail and held his hat down against the wind. "Why tell me all this?"

"What's the most valuable thing to have? And I don't mean in here." Taran gestured to his chest, pointing to the heart beating inside. "What do you consider the most valuable object to have?"

"Gold," replied the Captain, without a second of hesitation. "Some of my soldiers would say land or women are more important, but they're wrong. You can never have enough gold."

It is worth noting though, you can have too much gold. But Captain Radial was a captain first and economist never, and thus unaware of how an abundant gold supply would deflate the value and make it worthless, turning it back into a soft and heavy metal useless for almost anything one could want metal for. Except for jewelry, which wasn't much in fashion in Astria. And circuitry, but nobody on that planet knew how to make that.

"If," Taran proposed, "If the Ring had some of these resources you love, these metals or perhaps cotton or sugar which Lunate says you also love..."

"Yes?"

"Would you be so disinterested in the Ring then? Or would we have a harsher welcome, since we couldn't defend ourselves."

"Well," Radial scrambled to think of a softer way of phrasing it. "There is a country to feed back home." He left it at that. "Why worry about what could have been?" Or what could be at the Island, thought both of them.

Taran smiled and gazed out at the north, but that's not where he really looked. "Don't think much of it. It's just... With all these changes in the world, I'm wondering where it's all heading. What type of world should I be helping to create. What I'm reaching toward."

The captain nodded. He found the questions interesting, but irrelevant. Radial had decided those answers years ago as a child, following the footsteps of his family into the navy. Though he'd had setbacks and made mistakes as all humans did, his belief in himself had never wavered. "You head off now. We'll arrive safe and see what future we'll make then."

Taran agreed and headed below deck, determined to see what he could do to help. The captain stayed where he was, determined to enjoy his free time. He faced the deck, enjoying the sound of waves crashing against the hull and the blinding clouds in the sky.

Because of that, he didn't see the splash coming. He whipped around, his hat still on his head and the feather sweeping through the air. The stormer who'd taken the dare faced him, her tail brushing the water as she skipped along, her head at the same height as Radial.

The kid leaned in closer and narrowed her eyes to better see Radial's face. The Captain, his face a foot away from the wet stormer, smiled at what he perceived as a challenge.

Radial gestured behind himself at his crew with the hope they'd back him up and start throwing harpoons.

Reactions from the crew were mixed. Half began screaming for harpoons, half scrambled to bring up sailors from below decks, and half ran to actually get the harpoons.

While the sailors passed harpoons between each other and readied themselves, the stormer raised herself higher and peered at the others.

The first harpoon missed. The second didn't, thrown by the Crusader Lunate. It scraped the kid's right eye, and she disappeared back to the waves. Though they turned and twisted to see where she had gone, Radial and the crew couldn't find her.

"Coward!" shouted Radial in jest.

Below the water, the other stormers greeted her. She pushed past them, no longer playing but also not mad. Her injured eye kept itself closed while blood dripped between the eyelids to muddy the water.

The stormer wasn't mad. Just puzzled. Didn't these animals know their place? Well, the kid decided, they'd learn.

* * *

Taran ran above deck to find Captain Radial brimming with confidence and rearing for another fight.

"Great to have you here Taran. The way I figure it, you can go fishing for some bait and we'll lure ba-"

"Hold on." Taran tried slowing the Captain down to get the full picture. "What happened?"

The Captain tilted his head. He had high energy and high hopes and wasn't in the mood to slow down. "Didn't you already hear? A beast approached the *Saint Carpal* and flew straight up to my face. I couldn't turn down its dare like that, so-"

"But was she intelligent?"

"Well, it…" he trailed off as he noticed Taran's choice of words. "How can you tell its gender?"

"Intuition." That is to say, guesswork.

"Well, in any case, it seemed intelligent. Seemed to be able to pick up on my emotions, though it didn't seem combat minded. Coward." The captain pressed on, "So, go use your knowledge and get us some bait to catch that overgrown eel. Capitate, where are you?"

The corresponding sailor moved away from the rest of the crew, who had started arguing over who threw the harpoon and placing bets on who'd nail the stormer. Capitate had long hair strung in a ponytail and a goatee, and strode toward them, attentive and ready for orders.

"Capitate, you're up for fishing," Radial ordered. "Follow whatever instructions Taran gives you and get bait. That's all."

The sailor nodded, standing at attention as the captain strutted away and began preparing the crew for another sudden visit.

Under Taran's direction, Capitate hoisted a small boat down the side of the ship, filling it with chum in a bucket, a pole, and string. It was a bit strange when Taran asked for food and water to be added, but Capitate said nothing. He assumed it would just be a long trip.

The two set out to sea, far enough from the ship to keep in eyesight but the ship shrunk in size. From their new perspective under wide-brimmed straw hats, the ship would fit inside the palm of a hand.

The two passed time without comment for an hour. Capitate fished and kept the string and hook well-laid, but they still hadn't caught anything. The two assumed it was due to luck, but down below beasts and critters alike eyed the bait and disapproved of its erratic movement and the string attached. Capitate had tried to disguise the trap by jerking the bait as he reeled it back, mimicking sea life's movement. And it would've fooled most fish, that's certain.

But instead the waters of the Island held minds too sharp to be fooled that way. So the creatures of the sea ignored it, and instead chased prey that wouldn't stab their mouth in an obvious trap.

Neither human knew the futility of their attempts, and continued fishing. Taran stayed silent for long, and that silence disturbed Capitate. Not because Capitate loved sound, but because Capitate was observant. They'd noticed how often Taran bustled around the ship, making chatter or trying to help. The absence disturbed the fishermen, so he spoke up.

"The *Saint* can handle herself." While Capitate talked, Taran glanced at him and didn't contradict him. "It's one of the finest ships Astria has ever had, with a brave captain. They'll complete the hunt. And we'll have helped them do it."

"Maybe not," Taran said. "I'm not worried about our success. I'm worried how badly we'll fail." On cue, a slight drizzle began to fall. The shadow of rain clouds slid over the water till it reached the little boat. The drizzle pattered against their hats and continued onward in the direction the two had come from.

"The beast killing one of us, is that the worry?" asked Capitate.

"No. It's them destroying all of us."

"Them, as in, many of them? An animal wouldn't come back for revenge after it's hurt. I've been in enough hunts to know. Animals don't make plans like us humans do."

"An animal wouldn't plan like that. A beast would."

The rain's effect on the ocean was mesmerizing, droplets pounding against the waves to create a surface that seemed to be popping into the air. But the sound didn't calm the two men.

Big omens of the storm to come passed by, but neither human could perceive it since the omens swam deep below their eyesight.

Trouts, hydras, seals, whales, octopuses, albacore, they all swam deep below the boat, ignoring it and each other in a mad rush away from the Saint Carpal. Their panic consumed them, and while later the stampeding creatures would turn on each other, for now they were united in their fear of death and storms.

* * *

At the helm of the *Saint*, Radial held his hat down and looked out over the gathering storm. "Never seen one build this fast." he observed. Most of the crew had been ordered off harpoon duties to prepare the ship for the high winds and rain to follow.

There were still a few with harpoons at the ready though, so when Radial spotted the Stormer again at the bow—now with a real challenge in her eyes—the Captain smiled.

"I take back what I said about your cowardice, my lady." He bowed with a jeering smile, then snapped up straight and shouted, "Attack!"

Events start accelerating from here, followed by much screaming and wreckage, so you need to understand why stormers are feared among the beasts of the shallow ocean around the Island. Stormers live in schools together, and the adults can grow to the width of a house and the length of five school buses.

Individually, they would not be much of a threat to the Island itself, but for humans, they're a terrible danger. The threat comes from how they rile up the sky and the ocean into a frenzy, then feed on the remains of the resulting destruction.

When the young stormers had returned to their school after the prior attack, the adults' admonishments for wandering off turned soon to anger at the kid's injury. So began the crusade.

As sailors threw harpoons, stormers dived from the water to snatch the weapons, then dove back under water. For this one expedition, the school had appointed the young stormer the conductor. While the control over it all exhilarated her, the elation didn't last forever. The sailors kept throwing harpoons, but now that she was wary, she dodged them all. Spitting in rage, the stormer headbutted the Captain. To her it was a thump against her skull, but to the Captain it knocked the air from his lungs. He wheezed against the edges of the deck, his hand on the rain-splattered floor as he tried to push himself up again, only to fail.

Observing it all, the young leader began to waver. Not out of sympathy. She had started this with the intention to massacre the crew and trash the ship. But looking at the weak smattering of humans before her, she began to feel hate that she'd been stabbed by one like these, and also confusion—a feeling that this wasn't a good enough punishment.

So she ignored the *Saint Carpal* a moment and dove underwater, then circled around the ship and noticed the far off boat fishing in the distance. She twisted around to peer at the similar boats on the sides of the ship offering leave for the sailors. Then her plan unfurled.

Underwater, she coordinated the idea with the school, picking the nimblest young ones and having the adults waiting on standby.

With the kids, they flew through and around the ship, picking up all the crew members. The young stormers were small enough to fly with wind through the passages in the ship and grab any stragglers. Though many tried to resist, they all failed.

One clever sailor inside the ship was asleep and heard the shouts of protest, then barricaded his door with a chair.

However, the stormer only needed a second try to break it down.

Another sailor and explorer, Lunate, read to himself in the captain's room, hoping to enjoy some quiet time. A knock at the door startled him. "Yes, what is it? Can you come back later, I'm having a good read." This argument, riveting though it was, did not convince the stormer, who broke through and snatched Lun.

All weapons were knocked out of hands, and the sailors were dropped into untethered boats, dropped into the water. The leader grabbed the captain personally and set him down, with a smirk on her face the captain recognized.

The entire crew, now on boats, patted and checked each other and were astonished to find no injuries whatsoever. Unless you count minor bruises from being dumped and dragged. The conductor's order had been clear. True pain would visit in a different way.

An adult stormer swam to the surface and nudged the boats far away from the *Saint* with gusts of wind and waves.

When all the boats, including the fishing one, were now in shouting distance of each other, all attention went to the stormers, who began their ritual. The entire school began swimming clockwise around the *Saint Carpal*, speeding up like if they'd created new currents just for the event. Above, the storm accelerated and adopted the same clockwise spiral. Below, the ocean glowed and crackled.

A lightning bolt hit the ship, the thunder a herald of the chaos to arrive as the water below and clouds above exploded and raced to embrace each other.

The result was a violent spiral of water, clouds, lightning, thunder, and stormers—a pillar of destruction against which few beasts could withstand, not to mention a ship. The role of the stormers in all of this was to swim on the spiral's edges and keep the storm going while they took hit and runs on the prey caught inside.

The prey didn't stand a chance. Masts snapped, hulls ruptured, colorful sails designed to master the wind were torn to shreds and reduced to scraps of cloth. The *Saint Carpal* groaned in her last moments, but couldn't survive. She perished before the spiral ended, blown away into splinters and the occasional knick-knacks of the crew who had once maintained her.

The rage of the school and elements subsided soon enough, and they dipped into the water, now tired but satisfied. Only one stormer hesitated, the leader. Before she dived back in, a feather brushed her. She found the naval hat and exotic feather of the captain.

She remembered that fact, and nudged the hat until her lightning sizzled it into oblivion. Now truly satisfied with her humiliation of the crew, she sailed back down toward her home.

2

A Flipped Coin

Despite the utter destruction of the *Saint Carpal*, the entire crew was alive. The worst injury any of them had were bruises, so there was little reason to complain.

That consolation, unsurprisingly, didn't comfort most of them as they paddled and sailed their way back undisturbed to the Ring. Their mood didn't improve when they kept on and felt the air growing colder as they returned south. The crew had not brought their cold weather clothes along when the *Saint* sank.

So it happened that the Astrians and Skulks on the Ring went out to greet a shivering and sour group of sailors who huddled in cloths stowed on the boats, holding up their meager salvation like tents to protect against the blinding cold.

The rescued but humiliated crusaders waddled past the other ship moored on the coast into the village of the Skulks. A narrow river cut through the land, from the sea surrounding the Island, through the Ring, and into the wider oceans of the world. The village didn't tower or sparkle, but it never failed to shelter the people who'd erected it. The buildings were either tents of pelts stitched together or igloos, whatever could keep in the heat of burning oil lamps. The center featured an ornate building, low to the ground and the finest dome in the village. On its frigid walls etchings showed wavy lines for the wind, claws and shapes of fearsome animals, and figures of humans to rise to the challenge. The outskirts of the Skulks, beyond a low ice wall to break the wind, was a cave for burial.

Best to focus for now on the Center, the fallen explorers decided. Inside, Astrians had added their own decor with crates and supplies littering the area. Stations and desks had been arranged in the corners, past bestial heads and stoic sculptures carved on the wall. Fat oil lamps hung from rings on the ceiling, letting in more light. While sailors crowded around the tables inside to warm up or help injured comrades, the Captain of the second ship, Ulna, gathered Radial and Taran to explain what had happened.

Taran didn't want to be there, he'd rather have gone to see his family, but the second Captain, who was still warm and confident and not all that concerned with their feelings, had insisted he stay to help explain.

A word first about the second captain and co-commander of the voyage.

Captain Ulna was the captain of the *Phalanx*, a ship dedicated to combat that had chafed at the lack of such demand so far during the trip. Ulna prided herself on her wisdom, patience, and regal appearance. She didn't have something as sweeping as her comrade's hat, instead going for an intricate uniform bearing tassels and excessive details. The main color of her uniform, navy blue, mixed with dirty blond hair and height to create a visage that helped hide occasional slip ups in her composure.

That's how she managed, after hearing all the events that had unfolded in the first chapter, to not convey her chaotic thoughts to the duo when they'd finished telling her what happened.

Captain Ulna's first thought was to go get revenge on the stormers. Her second was that the Astrians now had one ship left, and if that one got wrecked, they would be stranded with no way home.

She had to scrap her plans to explore the other areas of the Ring, and she decided she wanted to punish Radial.

"I've decided I want to punish you."

"But we all came out alive!"

"With all due respect," Taran pointed out, "Our survival wasn't because of you. Us being in trouble, now that was."

"Da, eh, uh..." Radial's brain short-circuited while he tried to process when he had ever been humiliated this badly. Since he couldn't remember such a time in his adult life, he kept stammering, so the others continued talking. It might seem strange that Ulna could punish Radial, since both were Captains of high ships. But in Astria's aristocracy, Ulna ranked higher, and had been a close ally with the emperor for decades. Plus, she had handpicked Radial as her entourage. He didn't want her to regret the choice, and also didn't want to draw attention again to how his ship now lay strewn across the ocean floor. So he kept quiet. She could, and would, punish him if she decided.

"Is there any way to send a voyage to the Island?" asked Taran.

"Well, you know, here's the thing." said Captain Ulna. "As much as I'd like to keep supporting these joyrides to explore the North pole, we have one ship left. If that sinks, there's no way to get home. Astria will probably assume we got lost at sea. So no, I'm not risking it."

"What if I and one other person sailed there on a small boat?

If that sunk, it wouldn't be much of a loss, right?"

"True." agreed Ulna, before her suspicious mind kicked in. "Why do you want to go?"

When Taran started to answer, she cut him off. "Right, same reasons as Radial—glory and all that. So, now to—"

"That's not why." Ulna didn't appreciate the interruption, and showed as much on her face. Taran kept talking though. "I want to reopen ties with the Island, since they isolated themselves decades ago. I've never been there, and with how much we, the Ring, revere the Island, I want to see a connected world again."

"Hm." Captain Ulna didn't respond to the reasoning, instead thinking privately that the Skulks and Ring could certainly use some cross-cultural travel to spruce up the small and, in her eyes, primitive land. "So, who to send..."

"I think—" Radial piped up.

"No."

"But..." he trailed off at her disapproving stare.

Ulna leaned back and observed the hall. Her gaze didn't focus on much, instead browsing the sailors and soldiers. None met her gaze though, including the Crusader next to the group, who scribbled quickly in a notebook bound in leather, with a white quill that ended in black feathers. As his hand ran the ink across the page, a bare necklace jangled on his neck—a simple leather string with a charm attached—of a tower carved from amethyst.

"Lunate."

The Crusader glanced up. When he saw her full attention on him, Lunate closed the book, screwed a top onto a small glass inkwell engraved with random letters, and set his writing instruments on the table. "Yes, Captain?"

Her hand flicked at Taran. "Want to go?"

19

"Yes, of course." Lun straightened his short hair and ruffled his mustache a bit. The next part surprised Taran, as Lun spoke to him in Skulkian. "It's a pleasure, sir. Do you remember much of me?"

"You've been talking around a lot, to much benefit, I see. And you were with us on the *Saint*." Taran smiled, though it faded a bit when he noticed the Captain's puzzlement, so he switched to their language. He was glad to be addressed with respect, but he wondered if Lun had talked in Skulkian just to show off. "Are you strong? How good are you at combat if we meet any hostile beasts? And what about sailing?"

Lunate kept it humble. "More than enough to support you. You see, I'm a Crusader. Few in number, we're trained in everything an explorer could need. Survival, combat, navigation, scholarship. Although, for this voyage, I think we'll need above all diplomacy and intelligence." He smirked and tapped his head.

Captain Ulna didn't add to the list. Even though Lunate was so skilled, since he had no property or wealth of his own, she thought him little. But she did agree to Lunate, he had one thing she valued much. Loyalty. She said, "Glad to see you're so confident. Taran, do you want him?"

The Chief nodded. "Glad to have you with me." The two shook hands, bolstered by how little they knew of what lay ahead.

* * *

Now back with what was left of his family, Taran flipped a coin to his granddaughter, a child in heavy clothes who had just learned to walk. She resembled a penguin as she reached for and missed the coin, then waddled after it. Taran steadied the little girl as she almost fell over. Despite Phoca's inexperience with walking, she remained determined to dismantle the pelt tent and everything in it. Vitulina kept cleaning up the child's messes, but never seemed to mind much.

After Vitty shuffled some bone knives away from the girl's view, Phoca focused on the sparkling coin Taran had picked up again and twirled between his fingers. She reached for it with stubby fingers, foiled by the coin disappearing between his fingers. Her frown didn't deter his smirk. From the two closed fists the Chief presented, Phoca chose the left one. Her frown deepened, and deepened again when Taran's other hand opened to reveal no coin.

The old man laughed, and then shook his arm to shake the coin out of his sleeve. Phoca snatched it up and grinned, stumbling away to examine her prize.

Vitty shook her head. "She could choke on that, you know."

"Please, my granddaughter's smarter than that."

"If you say so..."

The two didn't speak for a while, instead playing with Phoca. Inside the tent were three generations, left lonely by the losses of an unimmunized population. Taran, his daughter-in-law Vitty who'd married Natar, then Vitty's daughter who stumbled after a sparkly coin.

"Why can't you send someone else?" Vitty complained. "You're the Chief. Pick anyone."

"Recently elected Chief. I suppose I still have a want for an adventure." Taran didn't have to ask what she wanted, he could pick up on it. "You'll make it through while I'm gone. We'll stick together."

"Still, the Skulk's chief shouldn't be off on adventures. Maybe this is a sign that you should stay with us."

"Sorry. Tell you what, when I come back, I'll stick closer to the Ring. Maybe not always in the village, but at least close enough to be able to govern. Say," said Taran, steering the conversation, "how are those iron tools working out?"

"They're um, quite good." Her mood picked up as she focused. "Much more durable than bone. And iron seems to cost almost nothing where these sailors come from. Trade with them is turning out well so far. Mostly we keep to each other, but some from both sides are trying to learn the language and bridge the gap. It's quite the change."

The Chief smiled and looked at the ground, tearing up un-expectedly. Vitty looked away before the two hugged. The two weren't sure of everything that had happened and would happen. When so much bad had happened in the past, could the future be made any better? Phoca didn't understand, and stumbled forward to wrap her chubby arms around the two.

Vitty laughed and picked her up. "Go to the Island, and do your best. The tribe will be fine while you're gone. Good luck."

3

Two Cords, A Package, And A Dash Of Hope

On the mythical and mysterious Island that so many people were trying to reach, there was a girl. She had no magic or special responsibilities outside of helping her family and the people she lived with. She had friends and games and a village that had undergone quite the change lately to make itself safer.

None of that satisfied the girl, whose name was Abeke.

But first, a word about where she lived, as you may misimagine it.

Picture a circle. Two axes intersect in the middle of the circle, splitting the shape into four equal parts. That circle is the shape of the Island, and each fourth of the Island is a different place to be. Opposite Abeke's area was a mountain range. The other two places were opposites—an arid desert and frigid tundra. While the entire Island held marvels, those areas did not have Abeke, so their description is not included here.

The piece Abeke and her village occupied embraced green and brown—a mad fusion between pine forest and tropical jungle, but not quite the same as either. And the vegetation held even trees seven thousand feet tall. It all came together to make an environment where very little of the life stayed for long near the ground, such as the village where Abeke lived, which had been near the ground, but then decided it too dangerous to stick around.

On that day, the day of the week allotted to children to rest and play, Abeke's dissatisfaction led her to not do those things. While Maya found it strange that the energetic girl would spend time inside their house weaving strands into an apparent basket, she approved of menial housework and congratulated the girl. The impromptu basket was a basket, just not for holding what Abeke's caretaker thought it was for. So far, its structure had turned out close to Abeke's imagination. She drew her eyebrows together in concentration, keeping her work in front of her on the table. Not much light entered through the windows, but that wasn't the light's fault, as it had to pass through millions of miles of space, an atmosphere, a thick tree canopy, and past many beasts and branches before it could reach the girl weaving on the table.

Abeke, despite her determination to finish, stayed frustrated at being inside. So it came as a relief at last when she finished her creation. The girl had never seen a sled for sliding around icy wonderlands, so she'd created one based on what she'd heard, starting from the design of a wide, handle-less basket, then modifying it to be much wider.

It would make a terrible sled, but she didn't know that, and so felt proud.

In her happiness, she rushed outside barefoot, then almost slipped on the ice at her doorstep. The village was suspended in midair.

A few months back, Rollan had used his newfound help from

a friend to raise the entire village onto a network of platforms of ice, stakes set in the nearby trees keeping it up. Rollan had never studied architecture, and the first attempts had been horrendous. But once Rollan took Abeke's suggestion to add railings so children wouldn't fall off, everyone had been able to start enjoying the view.

Abeke rushed back inside holding her sled-basket in the air to put on shoes, and though they were just slippers of leather they did their duty.

She ran past the small courtyard of her house, then dashed to a walkway in the main center of the village, adorned with bigger wooden buildings not for living. In the middle of the frosty plaza stood a wooden pillar stretching high up to the canopy above with a spiral ice spiral stairway next to it. Detailed carvings of animals and faces had been etched into every inch of the pillar. However, since Abeke had seen the pillar all her life and knew its meaning, she ignored it. She climbed down a ladder on the side of the courtyard, still carrying the basket sled in one hand. With a hop she arrived at the underbelly of the chilly support structure holding up the village, a crude floor with beams set up everywhere. Abeke found Rollan where she expected, walking in between shadows checking on everything and running his hands over the things he'd built and now maintained.

In her excitement, Abeke started running toward Rollan and dove to the icy ground, sliding the sled basket under her. The idea had been to gracefully slide past Rollan or bump into him. Neither of those happened. The basket sled careened almost from the start. Rollan heard her in time and watched her flip in the air past him, where a soft pile of snow cushioned her fall, though she landed face first.

The snow hadn't been there seconds ago. But Rollan had

willed it to appear from thin air and cushion Abeke, so that's what had happened.

A word about Rollan. Like most on the Island and Ring, he had coffee colored skin. He'd chosen to add to the appearance his height gave him by adding braids into his hair. Like Abeke, most of his clothes were simple except for the rare claw or tail weaved into a shirt. And neither Islander had jewelry. But Rollan did wear a medal, which meant more than any piece of jewelry ever could have. The medal was smaller in width than the palm of a hand, and rested on a braided cord he wore around his neck. The cord went through a hole in the medal, with a rim of metal and a stained glass center depicting a snowy landscape under a bright sky, a beast on top of it—Rollan's friend, Suka—who stood proud, as a massive arctic wolf, with icicles cloaking her. The medal had incredible detail for its size, and a finer piece of art could not be found in all the world than the medals of the Island.

Rollan stood confused, unsure whether to be worried or surprised or amused. "Hey." He reached a hand down.

After a moment, Abeke puffed away a strand of hair in her face and accepted the hand.

"So, what's all this about?" he asked.

"I made it for you and the village. What do you think?" After brushing away the fluffy and damp snow, she held up the basket-sled.

"It's quite the basket..."

"It's not a basket. It's a sled. You always lit up when you described riding them in the tundra, and you missed them when you came back. So I made one, and thought it'd be great for kids to play with." Her enthusiasm paused for a moment when she glanced at the snow pile she'd needed to land in. She continued, though with a bit less confidence than before. "Then you could make slides and slopes, and um... stuff."

"Well, uh..." Rollan was about to answer when he noticed drops of water coming off beams of ice. Once he created something, it had all the normal properties of frozen water, which meant it could melt. So he had been making daily rounds to the underbelly to refreeze things and ensure the village didn't slide off into the treeline.

"What do you think?" said Abeke.

Rollan sighed, a puff of cold air coming from his mouth as he cooled the structure a bit. Then he sat down on a bench of ice that sprouted from the ground for them. Abeke joined him as he reviewed the basket.

After he had done this for half a minute with no comment, Abeke said, "What did I do wrong?"

"Well, a sled isn't just for fun. Pulled by the right help, it becomes a method of transport, and..." He rotated the basket-sled.

"It sucks."

"Well..." He glanced at her expression. "Yeah. It'd get worn down fast. It's not the right shape, and needs a better frame to hold it. Maybe wood. But then again I could just make a sled out of ice. Also, I forgot to mention sleds work best on snow, not ice." When he passed it back, she had no comment and stood up. "The design isn't your fault, if you'd asked I could've described it better. And you're an incredible crafts-person."

Abeke rotated the basket-sled, then threw it into the jungle below. If he'd decided, Rollan could've had ice grow to catch it, but he let it fall. "How am I supposed to help, then. How do I compete with..." She waved at the grand structures built around her, wished into existence. With a sullen air, Abeke sat

27

on the floor, her back leaning against the bench.

"Don't be silly. You can make cushions for the sleds or something so kids don't have to sit on solid ice." Then, sensing Abeke didn't just mean sleds, he leaned down and hugged her. She didn't cry, her sadness being mixed with a quiet anger. "Do you know how much everyone here appreciates you? You made this, after all." He tugged at the cord suspending his medal.

The girl, lost in her thoughts, didn't respond to his reasoning. "I need to go explore like you and make a friend. A beast who will share power with me." Then, since she wasn't one to shoot small, said, "Who are the strongest beasts on the Island?"

"Wow, what a question. Uh... What if instead I take you one day to the tundra, when you're older, to meet Suka. You could be friends with one of her pups, maybe? Or Rend! Maybe if you visited him more often and listened to his..." Rollan didn't much like Rend either, despite his importance to the village, and chose an inoffensive word, "ramblings, he'd consider being your friend. Or-"

"No, I want to be friends with the strongest beast on the Island. And no trick answers like saying the Chimera."

"Hm." Rollan breathed out, taking a moment to collect his thoughts as misty breath left his mouth in the cold. That ability, to breath puffs. He'd always enjoyed that. "There's no ranking. And with all the abilities different beasts have: tricks, traps, stormers, rams, bats, royal turkeys—there's just so many..."

"I know those ones already."

"Rend might argue he's one of the strongest, even if he can't fight. Maybe a mantis?"

"Where do they live?"

"Not so far away. In the caves. As for what they can do, no one is quite sure. They're antisocial. Frustrating. Although bats

28

hunt them, they're both monsters in their own right."

"Well, has anyone ever seen one?" Despite her comment, Abeke didn't mean to demean what it meant to fight a bat. The small things could ricochet blades of light at high speeds to tear through any predator or prey. Luckily for everything that valued being alive, the bats were omnivores and tended to use their powers in self-defense and to carve past tough plant shells for the fruit they craved inside. Though when they hunted, it meant there would be no need to cut up their food and chew.

"I know they're tough, because friends and beasts from across the Island have tried searching for them and failed," he went on. "If they don't want to be found, no one finds them. And they have tried a lot of ways. Since the sharpest noses, eyes, and ears have failed, it's safe to assume the mantises are good. Very good, and very much determined to stay hidden." He saw the way she was looking at her, and added, "No. I know that glimmer in your eyes. Choose a safer, more sociable beast to befriend."

Preferably, he clearly thought, a beast that actually interacts with people. He grasped his medal at that moment, looking down at the symbol of his friendship with Suka, something he'd worked hard to achieve.

"You're a great kid, and you'll be an incredible friend to a beast one day," he said. "Just be patient."

* * *

Abeke chose not to be patient. That wasn't enough for her. So that night she stood before an icy path with rails leading away from the village. Though a pack of food and skins full of water burdened her back, it didn't weigh down her determination. The forest had plenty of traps and tricks that would kill anyone not in the know, but she knew enough to not have to worry about that. In fact, she thought she could make it to the caves and back by the next night. Maybe even visit the ocean for how close it was to the caves. So she set off, with two recent creations in her packs; two braided cords. One for the medal she'd earn, and the other for the medal her future friend would receive.

* * *

Rollan turned away from the window overlooking the square and the Chimera's pillar, and decided to get to the point, focusing on the howler monkey with red cheeks walking around the large wooden room. Rows of shelves with pickled jars and tables strewn with tools littered the building. Some tables were large and strong enough to hold an elephant. The roof seemed strange at first too, a straw roof with a line running down the middle, as if the roof could be picked up and set aside if need be.

"Rend, would you take on Abeke as your apprentice, and later as a friend?" he asked.

The howler didn't respond, instead sitting on a nearby table and not paying attention. Soon enough, a mouth grew on the side of the simian's head. It smiled in a sarcastic way, before talking. "You guys are sweet and all, but no thanks. Why should I endear myself to her, when she clearly doesn't care enough for what I know to ask me herself? Also, have you considered she's run away by now?"

"Oh, she wouldn't." Rollan leaned back on the wall, trying his best to appear nonchalant and confident. "Sure, she's impulsive and reckless. Sure, Abeke once tested the village's foundations by hammering them to make sure it'd hold everyone."

Rend frowned while Rollan leaned his chin on his hand.

"You know," Rollan added, "it wouldn't hurt to close off the exits. Just until the food has to be gathered tomorrow."

"Sure, and as for Abeke being my stude-" Wind battered the side of the clinic-lab, and a blue bird claw flashed through the window to leave a note fluttering in the wind before leaving. "Ah, I thought she might've come to bring me to a patient. Ah well, what does it say?"

Rollan read through the note, scribbled in berry juice by a talon not used to writing. "She says that a friend of hers saw a small boat in the ocean, a little like the one that injured Ele a few weeks back." Rollan checked out the window, but the avian messenger had left. "I wish she'd stuck around to thank her."

"In any case," Rend said, "I remember that stormer back from when I healed her. So then, what do you plan to do about the people arriving?"

He read the note again, his brow furrowed for a minute. "Greet them, of course."

"Really?"

"Sure. It's not like they'll survive the trip here anyway, and things would be much simpler if they didn't. If they survive, we'll explain why we don't want them around and kick them out." Rollan shrugged. "We win either way."

4

A Makeshift Home

This boat was not one of the best of Astria's fleet. Though the proud vessel had streaks of green, blue, and black paint intertwining lines decorating it, it held space for just a few people. It currently held a Crusader and Chief who'd decided to embark on Astria's expedition to the Island, though Taran also claimed it as the Ring's.

As the night went on, maintaining and sailing the boat had occupied the two, but now their attention wandered as they maintained a steady course toward the Island—adjusting the rudder, tightening the sail, and cleeting ropes. The wind pushed against them, so they sailed upwind. Their supplies consisted of rations and equipment scattered around the boat in sacks; a machete, clothes, a heavy book titled 'The Spirit Of Adventure', thick leather boots, and the wide hats on the duo's heads. Lunate kept a cross-spear, his pride and joy, embossed with intricate entwining cords of gold and silver.

Taran, for his part, snoozed away the time, until he heard light humming from Lunate, who spent time away from the rudder at his notebook and ink horn, the small seal-able inkwell with a string attaching it to a quill.

Up for a bit of noise, Taran said, "Can you stop mumbling and sing?"

"Um..." Lunate flicked his eyes to Taran, then started vocalizing the notes.

"Come on, add words."

The words came, but not loud enough for Taran to hear over the spray of the waves.

"Oh," said Lun, "shouldn't we be watching out for beasts?"

Taran sighed and stood up, turning in a full circle to epitomize the emptiness of the calm sea before them, as they sailed under a purple and black sky glimmering with the full light of the stars. That might've seemed worrying, but since nothing had yet taken advantage of the bright night to strike, Taran didn't worry. He tilted his head, a speechless dare to the scholar.

Lun accepted, belting his lungs out in a display of reckless confidence in song; "Life on the sea is rough and strong, a hardener for the weary! It strikes and it steels, and makes its own way. Hail to the hardy sailor!" A couple more lines went like that as Lunate headed to the chorus. If the lyrics seem nonsensical, don't worry, dear reader. It's because they were. Though Lun used a sailing tune he'd heard crews use, his inattention to them meant he now made up the words as he went along. "Life on the deck is strict and awesome. Hail to the hardy sailors!"

Taran clapped for the climax of the chorus, set off by blood flying from Lun's cheek in a horizontal line, splattering in Taran's direction. Nothing appeared in the purple night to show what had cut Lun, no tentacle or shark or swordfish. As it was, the projectile had been so fast that it took a couple seconds for the pain to register and for the song-drunk sailor to raise his hand and touch his cheek, feeling the shallow cut.

Beasts began whizzing by at almost invisible speed, in the starlight they seemed silver bullets with wings. Taran felt one ruffle his hair before he dived to the boat's floor, and Lun followed a moment later.

The beasts, later visible to the sailors as they flew overhead, were flyfish. Or at least, that's the name the Islanders gave them—no relation to the sport flyfishing. Though it's worth noting how insane a flyfisher would need to be to fish these beasts. These flyfish had half the width of a man's fist and weren't thrice as long. Their silver bodies had pink heads and blue side fins that spread horizontal instead of vertical, like most fish. When fleeing predators, which they did then near the sailors, they shot across the surface of the water at high speeds. The entire school shot past, dozens of flyfish speeding a few feet above the sailor's covered heads. As they went past, one slower flyfish jumped slower than the rest, stabbing straight through the hull of the boat and leaving a small hole in it. Later, the sailors would notice it and devise a way to plug it, but for the moment they huddled and waited for the school to shoot past them.

After a few minutes, the two popped their heads up and inched back up to stand. They looked up at the undamaged sail, then looked down at the wooden hull's hole. Then they looked at each other.

"Quite the, uh…" Lun giggled and then sobered up. "Quite the adventure, huh?"

"Yeah, I'd say so," Taran agreed.

Taran handed Lun a scrap of bandage, and Lun thanked him and started patching his cut on instinct. His hands had tended injuries dozens of times in training, and did so without instruction, since Lun held nothing but shock when he realized that something, anything, could have hurt him.

Pass enough time feeling invincible around your own kind, and you might believe yourself to be.

* * *

The brilliant night lasted hours. The night's cycle amazed Taran as he sat on the boat's floor, keeping plugged up the hole left by the slow flyfish. He had used the machete's handle, but it was a weak fit, so Taran kept an eye on it. Lun, who hadn't lived with the Northern hemisphere's cycles as much, manned the ship with puzzlement as he watched Taran's awe.

"On the Ring," asked Lun, "The night only lasted a few hours. How are the nights getting longer the closer we get to the Island?"

Taran smiled with childlike satisfaction and recounted one of his favorite stories, "After the creation of the Island—may the Chimera rest in peace—both the day and night revered the Island and wished to watch over the aftermath of the battles that had happened there. While the day normally ruled for vast swathes of time to overcome the night—especially during summer—the day stepped aside for the Island. It decided that, at least over the Island, the night and day would settle their rivalry and share the space together."

The Crusader nodded, his mind thinking over the story even as he controlled the boat. Though he doubted the tale's truth, he noted to write it down later. Nothing could go unrecorded. He spotted greenery in the distance, the Island far away. "This night and day, are they similar to Lua and Sol?"

"The gods people where you come from worship?" Taran thought it over, then gave up and shrugged. "Perhaps. Would you tell me more about them?"

Lun started to, then looked over the side of the boat. Nothing in the ocean's depths revealed themselves. So Lun looked back and told his favorite story, though the old legends had fallen out of fashion in Astria.

It's worth noting, before I recount what Lun said, that just because he didn't see any beasts doesn't mean they weren't there. Watching. Curious. Many swam beneath the water, shadows and blurs in the dark looking up and seeing the boat blot out the blurry reflection of the moon and stars and purple-streaked sky. Plenty also flew far above, darting between the thin wisps that were the cloud that night, birds of wings made of clouds, and shapes that blended into the night sky. And while some beasts noticed the boat and wondered at the explorers, most beasts went about their business and went about their lives.

Back on the boat, Lun began, "So one day, Sol..." He lost his train of thought, and reorganized himself. "Sol is the sun. Proud and strong and shining across half the world. He sees us living under him, depending on his graciousness and warmth, and it pleases Sol to know his importance. However, skirting around him was his little sister Lua."

"The moon."

"Yes, the moon. Lua existed in her brother's shadow, shining in her brother's reflection. She was pretty but unable to compare to the pure power of Sol. She felt dejected, and though she always stayed near Sol, he never noticed her, so pleased was he with the world he sustained.

"Though the stars and gods consoled and praised her, she felt sad and wandered to the other side of the world. One day, on the dark side of the world while she stewed in her impotence, she noticed a creature calling out to her from the world below. A barn owl. Once the small owl saw it had her attention, it thanked her for the light she'd brought to help the stars illuminate the night. For the first time, she realized she'd reflected some of her brother's light onto the world.

"That was when Lua realized her destiny. So she started her cycles, finding the times each month when she could reflect light onto the world for those who had too little of it. The realization that she could help the world cheered her up. Though she visited her brother in the daytime sometimes, her brother's neglect didn't bother her anymore. She'd found her own life, her own purpose." Lun nodded. "So... yeah. Similar."

Taran noticed the slight nervousness around the Crusader about how his story would be received, a nervousness he set at ease by clapping with enthusiasm.

Lun bowed. "Thank you, thank you. You're too kind." He looked past Taran at the Island, close enough to no longer be an inscrutable speck in the distance. "Looks like it's about time we get ready to disembark."

* * *

As they got closer, disembarking seemed more of a fantasy than something they'd do that night. That Jungle quarter of the Island didn't have a beach, instead being ringed by thick mangroves that continued for a few miles before reaching land. The two realized this the closer they got to shore as the mangroves grew clearer and entered their sight. Lun sighed and picked up a paddle. He expected Taran to remark on his attitude, but found the Chief staring at the mangroves. "Something wrong?"

"Just..." Taran felt a slight squeeze in his chest. "I've never seen trees before. They almost seemed as mythical as beasts."

"Well, they're actually mangroves and..." Lun cut off, wondering at what it'd be like to see trees for the first time in your life. "But have you never seen plants before?"

"Just shrubs, prickly dry things. It's a struggle for anything to survive in the cold of the Ring, and with places like this in the world, it makes living seem effortless. Why, everything must be so abundant in places so overflowing with life that no one ever fights for food."

That got a small chuckle out of Lun. "It's not that easy."

"Perhaps not, but still." Taran breathed out a breath to calm his thoughts and focus. "Worried about what we'll find in there?" he asked.

"Well, after what we've seen so far, I can't say the unfamiliar territory is very appealing. What if some bird of prey swoops down on us?"

"And offers a platter of that fruit you Astrians love so much?" Despite the comment, Taran did enjoy the taste he'd gotten of the pitangas and plums, though he'd only had a few preserved ones brought by Astria.

Lun chuckled, despite his worry. "And what has you so cheerful about all this?"

"We're not about to turn back just cause we might get hurt, are we? Might as well find fun in it." Taran looked past the mangroves. Beyond the leafy trees stretching their roots into the water, the trees soon grew bigger until their number and height increased the farther inland they were, their tops even scraping past wispy clouds reflected in the dusky sky. At some point, Taran supposed, the jungle started rooting itself in soil, but that soil was so buried under canopies and foliage from where they were that the ground may as well not exist.

By the point that the duo were dozens of feet away from the mangroves, the two travelers had put on warmer clothes to match the climate—leather boots, long sleeved pants and shirts, while Taran kept on his straw hat, also courtesy of Astria. Both kept their accessories. The two kept their senses alert for any beast that might appear, and while approaching the mangroves, they did hear the buzz of insects and animal calls echoing throughout the forest—groans and caws and shrieks. But neither noticed the eyes glimpsing between branches watching them.

Below water lay a much bigger place, several dozens of feet of depth littered with seaweed and tree roots, thriving and pulsing with the creatures that inhabited it. One of those creatures took notice of the boat above, and went closer to investigate.Lun took down the sail and paddled between the trees. They each glanced occasionally down at the water, but the dense waterscape and dim dawn light filtering through the canopy kept them from seeing much.

Their smooth sailing didn't last long. As they sailed closer to the Island, wide paths between roots and trees became harder to find. When a path they followed became too narrow for a bit, Lun shrugged back his sleeves and grabbed the machete.

To explain himself, Lun said, "I know the hole will be left open, but I'm not about to use Sol, my cross-spear, to hack away at this bramble."

Taran switched into the role of the paddler, putting a pot loaded with food onto the hole and hoping it wouldn't let through enough water to sink the boat. That new arrangement lasted for a while, Taran paddling through the mangroves while Lun swiped every so often at roots and branches to open up a path.

This rough sailing lasted until the boat became entrenched on a path with roots so thick ahead that it would take Lun hours to chop through them. So now the two were tired and sweating while they wondered how far they'd need to backtrack. The boat's floor was flooded, though the shallow roots held up the boat. It wouldn't let them sink. The sun was the only consolation, having risen higher in the morning to let them work in light.

Lun's frustration mounted at the bow, as the trees blocked far-reaching eyesight, not allowing them to see how far they were from land. "The entire Island isn't made of mangroves, right?"

"No."

The Crusader looked back at the crowded path ahead, and whacked the machete deep into a root. "Any ideas?"

Taran considered the dilemma, his mind working it over as he noticed some beasts around them. Mosquitoes and plumper, darting bugs with glittering eyes flitted around the humans now confident that their necks were loaded with blood, and that the humans could swat all day and not match their speed.

The two were sitting down, frustrated and itching from the bugs, when a beast flopped onto the side of the boat. The manatee rested his flippers on the side of the boat, and kept most of his weight in the water, but even so almost toppled the boat. Taran and Lun held onto the sides of the boat while it rocked and stabilized.

Lun and Taran, both never having seen a manatee before and panicking that it might be attacking, scrambled to their feet. Taran slipped on the doused floor while Lun reached for the machete. The blade didn't dislodge, instead remaining stuck in the tree.

"Lun."

"Yes?" Lun said, about to bend over to grab Sol.

"He's not attacking."

"Oh."

Their panic subsided when the manatee didn't make any other moves, instead watching them curiously, and trying to not tip the boat with his weight.

"Hello." said Taran. He wasn't quite sure what to do, but a greeting seemed appropriate.

Lun joined in and nodded his head toward the manatee, a large beast with small flippers compared to his size and large horizontal tail. Dark green moss grew across his back. The manatee, for his part, tilted his head and twitched his whiskers, feeling out their response. Satisfied that the humans he faced were docile and unlikely to attack, he patted the boat with a flipper. A question.

"What is he doing?" Lun asked. He picked up a discarded paddle and held it over his head, making the manatee flinch back. "Want me to spook him?"

"Lower the..." Taran turned around and motioned at Lun to drop the paddle, which he did. Lun hoped maybe the manatee would leave.

The manatee, calmer now, patted the boat again and repeated the question. No, he didn't have any obvious way to communicate like writing or speaking. He left that to the louder animals on land. Instead he used gestures and poses and hoped the humans were perceptive enough to get it.

Taran spoke up. "But we need the boat." Then the Chief peered north to the obscured land, blocked by roots just coming above the water. "Or at least we did need the boat."

"He wants the boat?" Lun didn't wait for an answer, his mind processed the news fast. "You can tell what he wants?"

Taran shrugged, his intuition a mix of instinct and deduction.

In the meantime, the manatee seemed to sense their indecision and waited for them to answer, though his flippers slowed, tired.

Taran said, "I don't know what he wants the boat for, but we should decline and get to work chopping our way north. Or trying to climb the roots or trees." Though Taran admitted to himself the prospect of slow, tiring traversal over an unknown distance didn't please his aging body so much.

Lun twitched his mouth from side to side. He looked from the manatee, to the clotted path, then back to the manatee. He walked closer and kneeled to face the creature at his level, though the manatee's breath almost made him reel back. "We can give you the boat. People on the Island can probably just make another one." For a moment, Lun doubted himself. He was, after all, talking to a strange animal whose intelligence he had no way of knowing. Then Lun steeled his resolve. "But in return, please take us to the Island. Perhaps you know some route we can use, or have some other idea?" During the plea, Lun added gestures to try and get his point across, switching between pointing to Taran, himself, the manatee, and the Island.

The manatee nodded as if he understood. He dove underwater and surveyed the boat, judging the best way to work with it.

Back above water, where the humans waited for a response, he rocked the boat. Taran and Lun kneeled close to the floor and held to the side of the boat. Before either of the travelers stood up again, the manatee swam underwater and distanced himself from the boat, facing north. With surprising speed he dashed forward and up, ramming the boat and pushing it into the air. The boat, and the beast, rocketed through the air a few dozen feet before landing in a pocket of deep water. Taran kept quiet and focused on the bruise on his knee while Lun finished screaming.

Taran looked back. "He's going again!"

The travelers clenched for dear life for the next jump. This process continued for a while, supplies juggling around the boat and the boat's hull long since opened. Not much water sloshed inside between jumps though. Even so, that didn't comfort the clenched humans. The manatee never missed a jump or landed them somewhere bad. He'd been chowing down on the plants of the mangroves longer than Lun had been alive and knew the mangroves better than his own back.

The journey took a couple minutes, during which the manatee made twenty jumps. When the boat reached land, both humans tried to stand on wobbly legs, before flopping down. The manatee nudged the boat to tilt, and spilled the travelers and their soggy supplies onto the wet and shaded bank.

The travelers flopped onto the ground, then dragged them-selves up to move their supplies away from the water, before again collapsing with a view of the mangroves in front of them. The manatee moaned at them, his way of concluding their business, before taking the much lighter boat away.

As the two lay on the ground with aching bodies, Lun said, "Jeez, we were only a tenth of a mile away from land. Say, do we have still have the machete?"

They looked around to confirm that, yes, Lun had left the machete embedded deep in wood. Lun didn't have the energy left to be mad though.

Taran grinned and said, "Quite the adventure, huh?"

That set the two wet and tired travelers into fits of laughter while they rested. They'd need the energy, since they'd used so much of it to just get to the Island.

But somewhere, Taran felt a little energy come back. Much was left to do. But he'd reached the Island. Taran plunged his hand into mud. No, the Island was no longer too far away to see. It was here, wet and squelching and all too real.

* * *

Before the chapter ends, it's only fair to tell you, dear reader, what the manatee, whose name was Chechi, wanted with the flimsy and colorful boat.

After nudging the boat for a while, he set it between some trees and then jumped out of the water, diving onto the boat and crushing it. Chechi untangled himself from the wreckage and began hauling sinking pieces to a space deep in the water between tight roots that formed a sort of shelter underwater with openings inbetween. Chechi took his time shoving wood in between the crevices, before putting the sail over the biggest hole and tying the structure together with the rope that had held the sail. The sail threatened to come loose until Chechi wedged the top in between tight roots, so it wouldn't come loose. Chechi couldn't make a knot, so instead took a knot already in the rope into his mouth and lodged it into a crevice between the roots.

The shelter wasn't perfect. The sail door flapped open often with the current.

But Chechi liked it. And that mattered much more to him than a watertight abode. Now accompanied by fish nibbling on the moss Chechi had on his back, Chechi entered his home and rested, satisfied and happy with his makeshift home.

5

Bait

The duo now stood and observed the dense forest from the shoreline. Lun said, with a faint hope, "I don't suppose your mother, rest her soul, gave you any directions?"

"Rest her soul?"

"Well..." Lun coughed. "Your mother told you stories some-times about the Island. Since you're old and such, I wanted to bless your mother's departed soul."

"She's still alive, you know?"

"Oh. Wait, she even survived the chicken pox we brought?"

"Yes."

"Right." Flicking his eyes between the jungle and Taran, Lun changed the topic, "So, how should we find other humans?"

Taran didn't quite know. Even at the shore, the canopy of mangroves morphed into trees, dozens of feet in the air, getting higher after that the further you went into the jungle. The highest trees in the jungle even reached beyond the low level of clouds in the sky, two thousand meters in the air.

As they looked on, Taran made a note to talk to his mother later and admonish her for leaving out so many details of the forest. Vines, smaller trees, flowers, and palms grew on the sides of trees and branches, clawing with each other for space. The sounds, chitters, caws, and howls of the Island remained a constant drone, never allowing them a silent moment. And the colors. The forest wasn't just shades of brown and green. The old fallen leaves on the ground were brown and black, flowers were white and purple, leaves were tinged blue and red. The most consistent thing about it was its inconsistency.

Taran, remembering what Lun had said, focused again. "No clue. Got any ideas for finding humans?"

"What about walking until we find something made by humans? Maybe a clearing or discarded objects."

The Chief considered that for a moment, and then realized its problem. "But if the forest is too big, we might run out of food and water before finding them."

"Not like there's a better plan." Lun shrugged hopelessly. "Let's start."

Lunate marched, his cross-spear held high. It didn't take long before he tripped over a gnarled tree root. Looking back at it, it was a thin raised brown checkered curve above the ground. He kicked it. It didn't budge. Irritated and petty, he swiped at it with his cross-spear. The root, truly a snake, raced up the cross-spear and wrestled it out of Lunate's hands.

As the black and brown checkered snake fumbled on the ground, Lunate pulled Taran behind him and raised his bare fists in fight.

"Lun-"

"I got this Taran. I'm a master in unarmed combat. This snake's got nothing on me."

To their growing horror, the snake rose off the ground, like a cobra, its head now high than them. The snake was too thin to strangle and nonvenomous. But clenched between its fangs was the cross-spear's hilt. The crafty serpent tried a swing or two. It liked its new toy.

Taran bowed and pushed down Lunate to do the same. Both glanced back up after a bit.

The serpent nodded and then looked at Lunate. He motioned at the distance, then motioned at Lunate and waved the spear a bit.

"Lun, I think he means to say he'll leave us be if we leave him the spear and you apologize again."

Lunate had two minds on the topic. One said that the crusader should just suck it up and leave. The other mind, rather bigger and burlier, said outloud, "Is he out of his mind? I'm a Crusader! I've had that cross-spear for years, it's a mark of pride and do you know how much money it co-"

The sleek spear-point at his throat stayed his tongue.

Lunate kneeled on the dirty floor, and lay face down in apology. Then he joined Taran in backing away slowly.

* * *

They didn't have to walk far before the swarm started. At first one mosquito buzzed near Lun's neck. He swatted it, and it died. Then the mosquito's cousins showed up, having heard something about a feast. Then the cousins told their siblings and the siblings told their parents who went on to gather acquaintances. From there came a lot of mosquitoes. At first their excitement surged at the prospect of two victims who couldn't set them on fire or spit poison, but disappointment mounted when they found that only the necks, heads, and hands of these humans were uncovered. So they left to make preparations, which the humans took as a sign of their surrender.

Oh, how wrong they were.

For the duo, things were going well enough. Their progress slowed because of dense foliage, which they had to move around or between, and solid wood vines blocking the way. Except for the brief mosquito assaults, no creature had given them any trouble. An angry hooting they'd heard once above them and a stick that crashed to the ground near them caused alarm, but otherwise the two were unbothered.

Then the mosquitoes came back.

See, whereas you, dear reader, are familiar with mosquitoes that cannot penetrate several layers of clothing, that is not the case for the Island. On the Island, mosquitoes added complements to their sharp needle mouths. They'd gone off and harvested needles from the dangerous venena tree, which covered itself in hollow needles that jetted out irritating and itchy poison, a trick they'd learned generations before Though the leftover poison in the needles had bothered the mosquitoes at first, time and evolution had eliminated those pesky problems and given the mosquitoes unparalleled bloodsucking abilities that passed all the armor, scales, fur, cloth, and skin of their victims. It also gave minor poisoning to the targets. But that didn't bother the mosquitoes, so the suckers kept on sucking.

So it was that the duo, earlier calm and collected, were now swarmed by dozens of mosquitoes determined to have their breakfast and drink it too. No matter how the two struck back, most of the mosquitoes ducked out just in time. Taran got one, to no grief of the others, but another mosquito he'd swatted seemed dead till it picked itself back up again, straightened its wings, and resumed the attack.

"You know," said Lun, as rashes broke out over his face, "I'm having trouble seeing why anyone would live here." The Crusader missed Sol already. Lun had been trained in nine fighting styles. None were designed for flying pests.

"Perhaps we just got the jungle on a bad day." Taran grinned, then grimaced as another mosquito pierced his arm. "Were the mosquitoes always able to pierce our clothes?"

"What does it matter?" Lun didn't concentrate when he said that, instead focusing on the swatting war. The two sped up, hoping that the pace would throw off the insects.

Unknown to any of the combatants, small beasts had started watching the affair, clinging to the trees.

"Isn't there anything we could do?" Taran said.

"Perhaps we could roll around in mud, if we found any."

"Mud?"

Lun barreled on, "But mud could get us leeches. Maybe..." The irritated Crusader looked up at the trees, not noticing the beasts who'd been watching and hid in time. he dismissed his suspicion, and thought on. Lun could recall several warding plants he'd read of in the past that could work. But the Astrians had not thought them worth bringing to what they'd thought would be a cold climate. "Those palm fronds up there. The big leaves," he said to clarify himself, "What if we used them as fans to get rid of the mosquitoes?"

This set the bugs in a panic until they calmed down when Taran said, "The leaves are thirty feet in the air. Even if we somehow climbed up, what machete would we cut it down with?"

"Dang."

This process continued on for a while, with the two stumbling through the forest while rashes spread over their limbs and torso and the mosquitoes persisted.

Meanwhile, the nearby trees held more beasts in the background than ever. The beasts hid from sight, but not because of the humans. There were six of them now, a pack of siblings. The beasts were small and furry, similar to lemurs but different the longer you studied them. Each one was the size of a raccoon, with white fur; brown and black stripes marking them with distinctive patterns. Their hands and feet held long fingers, and their long tongues lashed out with sticky ends. Their long prehensile tails curled around branches and vines as they traveled across the forest.

The first stickyfinger, with neon green eyes, had started following the humans a while back, then ran off to call his two brothers and three sisters to join him. They'd joined in the opportunity, tailing the duo as they flailed against the swarm. The first stickyfingers, crowned as the ringleader since he'd found the humans, gestured with his long hands to his siblings. The signal to start soon. Each understood, sneaking away and waiting in the shadows under leaves and between flowers.

Meanwhile, the humans had made no progress in their battle against the swarm.

"Okay," said Lun, tossing out his sixth idea, "What if we found a river and splashed around?"

"We don't know where to find a river," countered Taran.

"But say we did. Splashing around would probab-"

At that moment, the duo passed through a rather narrow place between brambles suspended in midair. As they pushed through it, the mosquitoes joined too, weaving around the foliage. A resounding three-toned whistle rang out, and the only thing the humans saw before the new assault started were bright and colorful eyes dashing across the brambles toward them.

All six siblings ran circles around and on top of the humans, confusing them while their real targets scattered before the hunting party. Each stickyfingers scooped up the bugs and stuffed their mouths silly. Their speed and the ambush allowed them to eat dozens of mosquitoes in under ten seconds. A few stragglers panicked and fled, only to be caught by long tongues the stickyfingers lashed out from six feet away.

At the start was a swarm, and then there were none. As the stickyfingers swallowed the last bugs, they perched on vines and kept their distance from the recovering duo. None of the beasts could eat needles, so they spit those out to a side as they finished their meal.

"Um..." Taran recovered from shock faster than Lun, sweeping stickyfinger hair off his clothes and spitting it out of his mouth. "Hello. Why did you do that?"

Despite taking more time to recover, Lun put the puzzle together faster. "The swarm is gone. I think they used us as bait."

The stickyfingers ringleader nodded, his neon green eyes focusing on Taran. Then the ringleader tilted his head, posing a question and holding a hand near his mouth.

"What are you asking?" asked Taran.

The stickyfinger puffed in frustration, then got shoved aside by a purple-eyed sister of his who tried miming. She held both hands near her mouth and gave a small cry. Then she posed the question again.

"Sorry," Taran said. "I don't know what you're asking. Maybe I know the answer, but I can't answer if I don't know the question. Lun, any idea?"

"Nope." He scratched itches he had all over, and said with

some irritation from the pain, "Well little guys, so long and thanks for the help. I need a break."

"No, wait." said Taran. "Hey!"

A few stickyfingers had started to leave when Lun said bye, but they turned back when Taran called.

When the Chief spoke, he went slow and tried gesturing to get the point across. "I don't know your question, but could you answer mine? Do you know where we can find any people? Humans, like us. Do you know one, or can point us in the direction of one?"

The stickyfingers chittered between themselves in high-pitched voices, remarking on the ineptitude of humans to get so badly lost. One smaller sibling with orange eyes commented that he had seen a small human north-west of here, right before his sister had called him over. The ringleader thanked him. Then the ringleader turned to the duo, and out of respect for their help as bait, pointed them in the right direction.

"Thank you." Taran bowed. Though he wasn't sure if stickyfingers knew what a bow meant, he hoped the meaning got across.

It did, though the stickyfingers didn't know what a bow was. The ringleader chirped in satisfaction and the pack of siblings scattered into the heights.

6

The Spirit of Adventure

For a bit, let's leave Taran and Lunate to explore the Island by themselves and focus our attention elsewhere.

Don't worry, it's just for a chapter.

The throne room we're about to see was a year in the past and continents away on Astria.

Astria was a sliver of land surrounded by bullies of countries, who had spent centuries taking turns stealing, partitioning, dividing, then fighting, over the country. No nation around Astria hesitated to march in and take what it willed, for every state laughed at the Astrians, said to be excellent swimmers and sailors and terrible at all else.

The throne room of the poor king. They say war brings wealth. Perhaps, but not for Astria, who always ended up on the losing side. The columns were carved and painted to be spiraling rivulets of water, they seemed whirlpools that held up the ceiling. Engravings of anguilla eels looked and swam toward the throne across the floor and ceiling. Behind the centerpiece, a mighty pink and white finned and winged beast adorned a mosaic window letting in light. It wasn't an eel, not anymore.

It depicted one who had swam upstream far enough to become a dragon.

Still, the statues were gone. The carpets, the curtains, the flowing river-rug of gold, all had long been sold or stolen.

The grand double-decked doors opened, Skapho pushed past them. Ulna, along with several minor nobles and merchants, followed him.

Skapho sat on the throne, brushing his basil green robes so he wouldn't get tangled on the intricate curves. Admittedly, even as this land's ruler, he still had his foreign heritage from his native land. It had taken Skapho time to tolerate Astria's culture. But he put up with it, he knew its importance to them. The design on his clothes of golden leaves, a bit out of place, reminded Skapho of his home. Plus, the gold and green shades went well with Skapho's green eyes. Two cords slipped around the short man's neck, the objects on them beneath his clothes.

Strange, thought the man. He'd been away for decades but never stopped referring to that place as home. But the man's life had prospered away from it. With his powers of blades of light, transformation, and fire, few cared that nobody could be sure where Skapho had spent his youth.

As the group arranged themselves to face Skapho, everyone knew the meeting was a formality. Skapho had read pages of essays from the group on their proposals and reasoning.

"You are an ambitious group of people," Skapho started, wanting to soften the blow. "Thought and care has gone into the proposals you've sent me. I thank you. But I cannot condone the proposal to send an expedition to the north.

"In a time when we need to limit how much energy Astria spends on frivolous tasks in order to build up our navy, this cannot be approved. Chasing myths and bedtime stories of 'beasts' and the such cannot be done. That is all."

If Ulna hadn't been there, the merchants and nobles would've bowed and shuffled out. But Ulna was there, and while she nodded in respect she kept her feet planted, her eyes showing the defiance she didn't speak out loud.

"Everyone out." said their ruler. Everyone left, except Ulna. None of the others found that strange. In the same way beasts could sense meaning, the nobles and merchants had sensed only they were to leave.

Without appearances to maintain, Skapho sighed and walked to one of the windows, overlooking the landscape with Ulna. She joined him. Whereas she looked out and saw serene rolling hills that sustained the capital and grew food beyond the city, reminding her of her family's summer home, Skapho thought the landscape had always been rather drab and uneventful. You could walk through a field and, except for snakes, not worry about danger. No need to pay attention to the surroundings.

"Why don't you agree?" asked Skapho. He could've used his authority to shut her idea down, but it wouldn't have addressed her reasons and also would have been disrespectful to the long time ally that she'd proven herself to be.

"I get your reasoning. That doesn't mean I agree with it. Accounts from travelers from over a century ago describe the Ring and Island, lush with land and food and-"

"Beautiful women, yes I've read the accounts." That had gotten Skapho the best laugh he'd ever had. "Those accounts... From which explorer?"

"Larry the loony and Pini the brave."

"Ah, Larry. Along with Pini the brave, yes, who also described the country Minis. Overflowing with gold streets and pounds of spice dumped on every meal, so he wrote. You remember when we asked the court of Minis about that?"

She did remember. Their queen had burst out laughing when she'd visited a few years back.

"So maybe travelers tend to embellish here and there." said Ulna, "What if they're right?"

"And what if they're not? Although, I'm curious, would you have taken any other Captain on this joyride?"

"Radial."

"Radial? A bit too hot-headed, isn't he?"

"Maybe, but ambition is useful."

"Well, enough of this. I'm sorry, but I won't have Astria spend energy on hopes. I'm sorry."

Ulna frowned but nodded stoically. Skapho kept his eyes on the landscape as she closed the door behind her. Looking over the hills dotted with buildings and fields, Skapho still felt a pang, even after decades.

Skapho missed his home, a place he'd long since left but had never stopped referring to as home.

* * *

Several months after that evening saw Skapho walking on a thin path between fields of wheat. With no one around, he wore simple shoes and loose clothes. He journeyed beneath the morning sun. For other people, the long journey would've had them sweating and collapsed. When asked about his lack of sweat, Skapho said resistance to heat was another blessing he received from the twins up high.

Skapho reached the house, alone in a field of wheat. Despite

57

its solitude and distance from the nearest village, the marble flowers and vines decorating the sides of the house showed that the owner outranked anyone within miles. The house shimmered with bright blue paint and white lines. A balcony adorned the second floor, shaded by a roof. The revered demigod knocked on the front door.

Trique responded fast, since he'd been on the first floor preparing lunch. He smiled. "Skapho. You're here for Ulna, I presume?"

By way of confirmation, Skapho nodded and went inside. "She's upstairs?"

"Yes, go ahead. Would you like bread with jam and butter?"

"That'd be nice." Heading up the stairs, Skapho found Ulna lounging on a chair on the balcony, a book shading her face. That book, The Spirit Of Adventure, had caused Skapho's visit in the first place.

"I see why you like this place." Skapho sat on a chair, overlooking the vista of wheat stretching in all directions across the occasional hill. "Uneventful, but peaceful."

"Interesting that you don't say you like my house." Ulna raised the book off her face, seeming none too surprised that the leader and demigod of Astria had come to visit. "I take it peaceful and uneventful aren't your style."

Skapho didn't respond. Why do it, when both knew the answer. "The Spirit Of Adventure. I gave it a read. Even interviewed the author too."

"Is that so?" She said, with a casual tone.

"Yes. I'd expected him to deflect my questions about his exaggerations of the Ring and Island. Like... may I have your copy? I left mine."

She handed it over. There was no bookmark in it; no hint that

Ulna had been seriously reading it. No need to anyway, she'd read it a dozen times before its publication.

"This passage from page twenty." said Skapho- eighty pages filled The Spirit, which allowed cheaper printing and distribution across Astria with the recent phenomenon of the printing press. That press didn't bother Skapho. After all, he'd used it to help throw the revolution. Ulna had even been the one with the idea to print revolutionary pamphlets and spread them around.

"Page twenty," continued Skapho, "which describes beasts on the Island freely blessing individuals who are 'worthy' and 'brave'. My favorite part is how vague these are. Everyone I asked on the way here said they'd receive a blessing if they went. Nobody seems to think that if they went failure might follow. I thought the author, when asked about these exaggerations, would try to justify them as real scholarship. He laughed, saying the amethyst tower bracelet he wore had been bought in a flea market, and wasn't the real deal. Asked, he confessed—with no pressure from me—that he'd been paid a bag of gold bits to embellish and encourage explorers to go to the Ring. Paid by you."

Ulna's confidence didn't waver. She'd seen Skapho mad before, and this wasn't it. So she kept calm. "Well, nothing wrong with supporting the arts, now is there?"

The self-proclaimed demigod sighed and didn't respond right away, instead averting his gaze to the fields.

"I'm not forcing people to buy The Spirit." said Ulna. "That's of their own will. And if enough people agree that expeditions to the Ring are a good idea, then maybe someone other than you can fund the mission. I'm wealthy enough that I just need a bit of popular support to get this done."

"No." Skapho had considered the decision the entire walk here. It hadn't been easy, because even before Ulna had brought it up that evening Skapho had considered sending an expedition to the Ring for years. "I'll give the thing my divine stamp of approval, as it were. Assemble a crew, get the preparations, choose whichever ships you want. Perhaps the *Saint Carpal* or *Phalanx*. Maybe both. How does that sound?"

Throughout all this, though Ulna grew more excited, Skapho seemed almost tired, or longing.

The Captain noticed. "Why did you change your mind? Really, that is. It can't be something as impersonal as not wasting Astria's energy."

Trique interrupted the moment, setting a tray of white bread slice with jam and butter and butter knives. Noticing the atmosphere, he left.

"It's complicated." Skapho looked at Ulna, at the determined eyes that had supported his efforts for years. "I'll tell you though. You deserve that much."

So he did, as they sat and munched on food before fields of wheat.

7

Ice

Back to Taran and Lun, and how they were doing. Following the pointed finger of the lead stickyfinger, Taran and Lun had started out confident. After all, what would it take to follow such simple directions? Turns out it was hard. Just by walking through the forest, they lost the direction by a few degrees. That doesn't sound bad, but since who they wanted to find was a ways off, they would've walked right past.

Abeke saved the situation, though. From where she ate, ripping open a spiky green fruit she'd brought, the sounds of stomping through the jungle reached her. With her knowledge of the forest, the sounds told her right away how inexperienced and clumsy whoever they were was being.

"Tourists." She looked down at the fruit, sighed, took one final bite then threw the fruit high into the air. A bird caught it in his claws and flapped away. Wiping her hands on a nearby tree, she went to the sounds. Even though she had her quest to find a mantis in deep and dark caves, she couldn't let these inexperienced travelers get themselves into more trouble. While plenty of traders and merchants traveled between the regions of the Island, tourists and pilgrims also came along from the yellow desert and the white tundra.

Following the loud crunches of leaves led her to Taran and Lun, a bit disgruntled and covered in rashes.

"You should've hired a guide." said Abeke. "Are you from the desert?"

The duo spun around, and appeared only a bit reassured when they saw it was just Abeke.

"Hello, little lady. My name is Taran and this is Lunate, mostly called Lun. We're travelers, and you're right." Taran gave a good-hearted chuckle despite his fervent rashes. "A guide would be useful. You're from here?"

"Yes. My name is Abeke. And..." She lost her train of thought, trying to think of how to help so she could leave them alone and get to the caves.

Taran picked up the thread. "You mentioned the desert? Why do you think we're from there?"

"Rollan, a friend from where I live, knows so many people from the tundras that if one came to visit, Rollan always went to help. So you're probably from the desert, or the mountains, I'd guess." Then she noticed they hadn't said where they were from. "Where are you from?"

Before Taran could respond, Lun stepped in and tapped Taran. Whispering, he said, "Considering the Island's isolationism, perhaps we could pretend we're from another region of the Island?"

Taran glanced back at Abeke. "She's a kid. What's she going to do if we tell the truth? And what if people from other regions call us out on our lies?"

Lun was frustrated and kept up the whispered argument, oblivious to Abeke tapping her foot and watching them. She didn't think much of the ordeal at first, then got to wondering what was going on. Though she didn't always think things through, something occurred to her. It seemed unlikely, but, "You're from the Ring?" she asked.

The two stopped bickering, and Lun opened his mouth to speak, but Taran nudged him to close it. Taran said, "Yes, we are. As travelers, perhaps you could be our guide for now?"

"Yeah, you definitely need it. How'd you even get to the Island?"

"On a boat." Lun said. "Did you think we flew?"

"I just thought the outside hadn't progressed much beyond spears and huts. But okay."

Taran didn't much like the comment. Nobody on the Ring could make large ships like Astria, but without boats his ancestors wouldn't have even been able to reach the Ring in the first place. Taran forgave her though, as she was a kid who had never traveled far.

"So," Abeke said, making up her mind, "I'll show you how to get to the village and then get back on my way. You're injured, and Rend, my village's guardian, can heal you up from those mosquito attacks."

"Thank you." Taran said, as she moved north, traversing the jungle much faster than either of the duo. Abeke didn't run, but where the duo clambered over fallen trees or around bramble, she slipped past like they weren't there.

Lun trotted to walk next to Abeke and said, "You don't mind us being from the outside, do you? 'Cause I come from even farther than the Ring. And with the isolationism and whatnot..."

"Oh, you're from the badlands?"

Lun caught up her logic right away. "It's a bit mean to call everything outside the Ring the badlands,. We've made quite a lot of inventions, you know."

"Okay. What's eyesholaysha... whatever you said?"

"Isolationism. That the Ring doesn't like outsiders." He wanted to say more, but Abeke spoke first.

"Oh, that. You two seem alright to me, if helpless. And I'll let Rollan decide about what will happen to you."

Lun nodded, but went on with what he wanted to say, "How can you believe the entire world is just badlands? Sure, outside the Ring few can compare to Guttio and maybe Minis, and Astria has seen better days. But we've built great buildings and statues and treasures." He didn't mention how often those countries kept stealing those treasures from each other,

"Geez, I didn't know."

"Clearly." Now, on his high horse, Lun continued.

Abeke listened with some interest, but mostly surprise at how emotional Lun was.

"Why, this amethyst charm on my wrist is a medal of—" he said.

"It doesn't look like a medal," she interrupted.

"What? I mean, a badge. Whatever! This amethyst tower represents my studies at the greatest center of knowledge in the world, and my ascendancy as a Crusader, a paragon of skill, learning and virtue." As soon as he said it, he changed the topic. Neither Taran or Abeke had any idea how impressive Crusaders were meant to be. "Minis would disagree, but boo them. What do they know? Astria is a developed and civilized country with astounding architecture, knowledge, the printing press, even a sewer system. And we boast a clock tower! Not many cities boast of a clock tower you know."

Abeke nodded. "And this stuff you build, how high do they go? As high as these trees?"

"Um, no." Lun coughed. By this point, most of the things he described didn't even have a word in the native language, so he just used the original words. This didn't help. "But they're magnificent structures. Buttresses, arches, spires, gargoyles, rampa—"

"Lunate." said Taran.

"Yes?"

"Abeke has no idea what most of those things are. Do you, dear?"

"Nope." She smiled. "But I'm sure they're every bit as neat as Lun says they are."

Lun reddened in embarrassment, then gathered himself. "Well, you could just visit Astria one day."

"Maybe."

The three went on, brushing past spiny bushes and following Abeke. When she turned, they turned. For the duo, the jungle filled every corner of its space with pretty but meaningless color and sound. For Abeke, every corner was a hiding place, a potential way to make something mad. She noticed claw marks on a tree and veered to avoid someone's territory. A yellow and brown animal curled across a tree, and she turned away from it. For most of the beasts of the Island, keeping at a distance from them encouraged mutual distance. Though, some beasts did make their living on closing the distance.

At the first buzz Lun heard, he panicked and waved his arms wildly. Turning around, Abeke expected something exotic. Thinking perhaps that Lun had lost his head by way of some peckish big beast. Instead, she turned to see a tentative mosquito buzzing around, joined a bit later by the mosquito's third cousin. While Lun panicked and Taran tried to figure out what was happening, Abeke smirked a bit despite herself. She'd had the same reaction to mosquitoes when she was four years old.

After a moment to let the mosquitoes grow complacent, she gave a resounding three-toned whistle. The mosquitoes scattered off, though they didn't flee fast enough to avoid a few stickyfingers that popped out of nowhere to catch them.

While the critters stuffed their cheeks, Abeke said, "If you guys ever have that problem, just do that. It imita—"

"Oh!" said Lun. "Taran, it's like those monkey things. Back then, it must've been asking us why we hadn't called them for help. And even if none of them are around, it still scares off the mosquitoes."

"You've met stickyfingers before?" said Abeke.

Taran said, "It was quite the encounter."

The stickyfingers finished and glanced at Abeke. She smiled and nodded in thanks, Taran copied her and motioned Lun to do the same. Satisfied, the critters bounced away.

Abeke said, "No wonder you have so many rashes. You must've been a mosquito buffet for enough stickyfingers to converge naturally. Now then, we're at our destination."

Excited, the duo looked around, their disappointment apparent at not finding anything except another stretch of jungle that appeared to them the same as any other.

Taran noticed a glittering behind a few trees. "Ice?"

Indeed in the middle of a jungle a ramp, white rails started on the ground and rose off into the treetops, all made out of ice. When the project had first started, Rollan had needed to catch Abeke, who had tried the ramp and slid off into greenage. Now the floor and rails of the ramp were ridged to allow traction.

"So," said Abeke.

"Why—?" Lun asked.

66

"Rollan can explain that. I've places to go. Just follow this for a while and you'll make it to my village. Ask for Rollan, he'll take care of you."

"It won't collapse?" asked Taran. There were beams and stakes lodging the ramps in trees it brushed past, but Abeke understood the uncertainty. Droplets of water has started dripping already.

"It'll hold. I tested it myself. Now, off with you and good luck." She turned around and started off.

Taran said, "Wait, what were you doing out alone in the forest in the first place?"

Lun had thought of that question already but assumed Abeke needed to gather berries or something.

"I'm heading to some caves to meet a friend. Bye." With that, she left them surrounded by a forest they'd never find their way out of. Their only option was the ice path that lay ahead.

"Well, we did great by ourselves, huh." said Taran.

"Let's just get going."

"Wait, perhaps we should follow Abeke."

"No." said Lun. "Taran, there's no need to be concerned for her safety. She may be a girl, but she's in her home court. She'll be fine. And we have our mission."

"But see, this can help our mission. This would be gentle-manly, true, but imagine what would happen if we just walk into whatever hub this leads to. We may be kicked out on sight. But if we help out Abeke-"

"We'll enter the people's good graces." Lun caught on quickly. "Very clever of you. Alright, let's do it. We can still catch up."

8

The Lone Mason

Backtracking through the forest past where she'd found the two, Abeke reached the entrance to the caves without a problem, having skirted past anything too cranky that day. Seen from ten feet away, all you'd notice about the entrance were reddish grey boulders strewn across the ground. Clambering over them and through them—while praying you don't stick your leg into a crevice—would let you discover the openings. Considering that the holes were the size of elephants, their hidden nature was impressive to behold. Maybe it had been natural, or designed by a crafty beast.

Abeke peered into the dark mouth and, despite her impulses pushing her forward, considered the challenges of going in. It'd be bad manners to enter someone's home without announcing your presence. She'd also be bumping around blind in an unknown cave. So she sat cross-legged near the entrance on a boulder, then shouted, "Hello! I'm Abeke! Mister mantis, will you be my friend?!"

She waited for about a minute, before wishing she'd brought a game to spend the time. She'd imagined the evening before, that a mantis would respond quickly.

Abeke felt sure the mantis did sense her. But the introduction echoing through the caves didn't ease his nerves, so he took a careful approach. Of course, others heard the shout too, critters with bright eyes and sharp diamond teeth who clawed through solid stone. After swiveling their heads a bit, they burrowed again in the hope Abeke wouldn't shout again. Although Abeke thought announcing oneself was good manners, she had not considered whether that announcement being shouted into a home was also good manners.

In the meantime, Abeke yawned, tired as she was in the warm noon, having skipped on sleep the night before. So she napped.

***

That's how Gong found her, having slipped out of a secret exit from the cave system. Standing from a distance, he inched closer. After a bit, he realized there was no trap and strided forward to look, puzzled, at the sun-drizzled napper. At ten feet tall, he towered over Abeke. He kept his two forelegs tucked against his body, while his four thin legs creeped without hesitation across the rocks. Folded against his back were wings, so close to him that they didn't seem any different from the rest of his skin. Bulbous eyes with rings of blue, red, and black allowed him incredible vision. His entire exoskeleton was black, with the lines around plates being such a light blue they seemed to glow. But no antennas, Gong didn't have those.

Even with his senses having confirmed, for the tenth time, that no other beast or human hid nearby, Gong still spun around and checked. Reassured, though still puzzled, he nudged Abeke with a foreleg.

A light sleeper, she sat up and said, "Oh, hello. Thanks for coming to say hi. I'm Abeke. What's your name?" She had practiced the almost psychic way beasts could communicate emotions. Not that Rend had wanted to help.

Gong.

"It's great to meet you." She got the message, and trusted Gong would get hers. His name came across almost as intuition, and almost through his movements. Though his speech wouldn't be too complex, at least for now.

Why?

"Well, I want to be your friend. Could we get to know each other?"

Gong didn't respond right away. He mulled over the feelings he'd heard from her,—of desire and friendship. Abeke picked up on his indecision.

"Let's at least get to know each other. Could you let me in? Later, if you want, you can kick me out."

Gong, now satisfied there were no tricks and astounded at the girl's seeming insanity, responded, *Yes.* He nudged into the cave's entrance, leaving Abeke to scrape behind him.

* * *

Abeke didn't ponder the problem of darkness until the stone walls were already surrounding her. Despite that, it worked out. Gong emitted a faint flow from his blue lines that cut a striking outline in the dark. The two continued on for a while, Abeke needing to move around stalactites, shards, and pointy things littering the tunnel. After all, this space had not been designed for humans. Gong waited though, and a couple of minutes later saw them through twists and turns into a room so wide that the illumination didn't reveal all of it. The underground system allowed the mantis to keep his home safe. Though the route was short if you knew the path, not knowing the right way would lead to hopeless wandering through obscure caverns.

Gong's home differed from the rest of the system. The walls and floor were smooth. Littering the space were crude sculptures, chiseled from hard rock and decorated with colorful minerals inserted into nooks. Some were trees, other beasts, others hordes of wasps, though some of those had legs strewn far from the bodies. Most of the creations could work as paperweights, others stretched in their size to be taller than the visitor. Reliefs had been etched into the floors and walls, showing inexperience and passion.

Instead of sparking a conversation, Abeke took another nap, using her sack as a crude pillow.

***

Gong fidgeted with his forelegs. His attention moved from the young visitor to his creations. Despite his anxiety to leave and hunt a bit, the worry that Abeke would damage something persisted. That may seem silly, since everything was carved from solid stone, but Gong had not met many children. The rumors that reached him said that children were unrepentant ghouls who destroyed all they saw. But, eager for a reason to leave, he figured that he'd leave and make this a test. If Abeke treated his cave well, then that'd be a good mark in her favor. So he left, not considering that it might be bad manners to leave her alone in complete darkness.

She dozed off into the afternoon. Refreshed, she awoke to find Gong back from the hunt, chiseling at a cube of obsidian checkered with emerald. She watched for a bit.

Mantises on the Island have blades along their forelegs. Blades are very real, cutting through anything, but look ethereal, almost as if weaved from hard blue light. They're small most of the time, but can grow to immense size. Gong had cleaned the blades from his latest outing so the sculpture wouldn't be dirty.

Unable to concentrate with Abeke's attention, he set the project aside and looked at her, unsure what to say.

"What do you want to make from it?" She pointed at the cube to clarify.

Small. Animal. Chunky.

Abeke didn't understand more than that, but assumed it'd be some beast in the shape of a cube. "So, I've been wondering. A friend of mine said mantises, and you, avoid humans and don't want to be friends. Why'd you welcome me then?"

Gong tilted his head, then held a foreleg to his head then lowered it to Abeke's height. *Small. Child. Harmless.* After a pause, he noticed Abeke's frown. He didn't know what a frown communicated but got the idea. *Not incompetent. Child.*

"Hmm." She moved on from that line. "Say, does nobody else live here? Is your family out?"

No. Solitary.

"Oh, I'm sorry to hear that."

Why?

"Well, it's sad to live alone."

Is fine. Alone, my way. Mantis way.

"Do you have friends?"

72

No... Others. I know.

"Huh. So, would you like me as a friend?"

Another pause as Gong considered this. *Friend. Why?*

"Well, friends are pretty great, even if mantises aren't as social as humans. Yeah, I'm not strong enough to help you hunt or something like that, but friends can do plenty of stuff. Like play-"

No. I mean... You. Why want?

"Oh. You probably ask that since I already have friends at the village. Kawm and Beni are great friends, You should meet them. So, why do I want to be friends with you? Can I be honest?"

Yes.

"I need help. I have a decent life. But nothing more than that." A frown crept onto her face. "It sucks that I just spend time around the village, spending time doing nothing other than weaving and playing. I hate it. If we become friends, you'll get companionship which isn't all that important to you anyway. Look at you, you can mince trees and carve through stone. But I'll get your medal, and become important and stop wasting my time. I'll be strong. Maybe just happiness is enough for other people, but not for me. So, yeah, it'd be great to be your friend, but I can't deny the benefits are a lot more for me. I even..." She pulled out the necklace cords she'd prepared beforehand. "Brought these along, in case you agreed. Never mind all that about sealing our friendship though."

She paused here, almost as if in pain. "It'll suck, but we don't have to be friends. You can say no and I'll leave. Never mind that, though. Let's see if we'd be good friends."

How?

"We could play a game. Do you know catch?" She grabbed a rough stone from the floor and tossed it up. Gong focused on it. By the time it reached the ground, he'd slashed so that the stone became dust.

Win?

"Kind of. Let's invent games later. Perhaps we can chat instead. Tell me about a recent hunt you had."

Gong, pensive, decided to play along while he thought it over. *Attack. Sting. Run.*

After realizing this didn't provide much information, he scraped together small figures gathered around the cave and prepared a show.

A mantis stood on the floor, defiant in its unmoving stance. It guarded several small round stones, and several wasps buzzed menacingly—lifted in the air by Gong, who tried to imitate buzzing with his mouth. Each wasp was almost the mantis's size, and the ensuing fight was brutal, figures bumping into each other as the mantis protected the round stones while aggressive wasps swooped in for attacks.

After a fierce battle, all the figures were swept aside. One round stone remained, which Gong raised up and swapped out for a smaller—relative to the previous mantis carving— figure of a mantis. Then Gong switched that one out for an even bigger mantis. This one, strong and as defiant as his predecessor began to creep up to a new arrival on the scene.

A mound of sand and dirt, punctured with holes and in no particular shape. Now and then, wasps shuffled in and out of the structure. After the obsidian mantis prowled around the hive for a while, he struck. He clashed against the hive, making terrible scraping noises and dropping into the replica, which Gong picked up and shook around to simulate a terrible battle.

Wasps dropped out of the hive every now and then, and soon the mantis dropped out. Gong righted the carving, where it stood victorious among the corpses.

Revenge.

Abeke tried to figure out what story Gong had told.

What think?

She clapped and smiled, her past mood now forgotten. "That was awesome."

Understand?

"Um. That last mantis was you, so the first one who you're getting the revenge for... Were those round things eggs? So the one who lost that fight... a parent?"

Yes.

"Wow. Do you ever show anybody all the things you make here?"

No. I... Gong focused on Abeke, his decision made. He brought his long forelegs together in front of Abeke. A medal crystallized on top of them, first as stars and diamonds until it coalesced into a physical object. The medal, lowered to Abeke's height, was small but so detailed it'd make any jewelry creator jealous. Obsidian flecked with sapphire rimmed the medal. The rim also held a small hole for a cord, with the medal composed of stained glass. Only two colors were in the glass, shades of blue and shades of black depicting Gong crouching in the shadows of a cave. Another medal crystallized in Abeke's hands. It had a wooden rim and depicted her standing on a branch far above the ground. The friends exchanged the medals, and threaded the cords to make the necklaces. Both fastened it around their necks. Abeke helped Gong fasten his.

"Thank you."

I might still decide to not be your friend. But I look forward to talking to you from now on. Friends help make each other stronger, right?

75

"That we do." Abeke smiled, happy to learn that Rollan was right about improved communication between friends.

Before you leave, let's head out. I want to see what happens when another creature draws on my help.

9

Lights In The Sky

In that afternoon, while Abeke made a new friend underground, Taran and Lun stumbled into the clearing with the reddish boulders. By this point both had gotten fresh scrapes and bruises. Lun said, "We would have been better going on that frozen death trap. We might have fallen, but at least we wouldn't be lost."

"Alright Sparky, complaining isn't going to help. Besides, maybe we're just about to reach those caves."

Lun spread his arms across the clearing with half a dozen hidden nooks and crannies. "Do you see any caves around here? Face it, we're in trouble. Our best bet is to try backtracking and not go astray again."

"Then that's what we'll do." said Taran, simply.

"Alright. Taran, honestly, you need to learn to get practical. This plan sounded good but was too hopeful."

Due to their discussion, neither ended up moving yet, both glad for a chance to rest. "Hope sounds nice."

"Yes, but the world chews and spits out naive guys with heads stuffed of hope."

"What would you know of that? I'm twice your age. What do you get out of lecturing me on how the world works?"

Before Lun could answer, they heard a crackling and a crashing in the trees. Both squared their arms, expecting another flaming pig, before something crashed in the clearing in an explosion of icicles and snowflakes. Rollan stood up, back in his human form. He observed the area before settling on Taran and Lun. "Hello," he said, "I'm Rollan. Who are you? Perhaps two hunters trying to find a mantis again?"

Lun started to say, "Wh-"

Rollan interrupted, and said, "Never mind, that doesn't matter right now. Have either of you seen a girl round here? Pack on her back, maybe eating fruit, in a hurry?"

"You mean Abeke." said Taran. "We just saw her a few hours ago. Did she run away from home, or something like that?"

"No, she's done something much more reckless." Rollan studied the boulders and rocky ground, which he knew to be hiding caves underneath. "Did she say where she was going?"

"To some caves to meet a friend."

"Of course she said that. So you decided to go to the caves with her. Why?"

Lun, having realized the situation on the fly, said, "Though she ran ahead of us, we still feared for her safety, so out of compassion, we followed her here, to the hidden cave entrances under these boulders." He paused a moment, to see if Rollan would contradict him. When he didn't deny Lun's guesses, the Crusader said, "How could we let a girl like her wander alone like this, in such a dangerous place? Since you're also looking out for her, let's join forces."

Rollan nodded. "Sounds good. I'm her foster brother, by the by. The problem for finding her, see, is that she's surely in the caves by now. I don't know the way inside, it's as winding and dense as a wasp's nest, and probably just as dangerous."

"So," said Taran, "Our best choice is to head straight in?"

"I think so." Rollan and Taran both headed toward the crags and began searching. Lun just stood in amazement to one side until Rollan found one wide opening, and began to climb in. He helped Taran in, and also volunteered to carry the old man's bag.

Lun inched closer to the entrance, and said, "This is a terrible plan. Who knows what could be in there?"

"We don't know," agreed Taran, "But it's the right thing to do. Are you joining?"

Lun did, then drew and lit a small torch from his pack with flint and a dagger.

"Thanks," said Rollan, "I hadn't thought about light." The three walked in, with Rollan leaving a thin trail of ice behind them to mark where they'd come from.

With the torch only to last for an hour, they set on their way. They had no idea where to go, so they just took their time navigating the forbidden corridors.

"Say," said Lun, "How are you doing that ice thing?"

"My friend is Suka, from the tundras." said Rollan.

"Tundras from the Ring?"

"No, of course not, from the tundras here, on the Island." Rollan took a closer look at the two, though all three kept walking on. "What did you say your names were?"

"Lunate, mostly called Lun."

"Taran."

"Right. Lun, your skin is awfully light. You from the mountain range? Or..."

"That's right," Taran said, "We're foreigners. I'm from the

79

Ring, of the Skulks. Lun is from the far outside, of Astria."

"Never heard of that tribe. Oh wait, I think Maya may have mentioned it to me in the past. Still, not that big a group. And never heard of that country either." He said these offhand.

Lun said, "Is that a problem, us being foreigners?"

"No. Or, it is, but that's not important right now. Let's just focus on finding Abeke for now."

They didn't find her. Their time ran out on the torch fast enough. On their journey underground, they'd found jutting spears of stone, heard scratches far down the tunnels, seen springs of water, but no mantis cave, or Abeke. Near the end of their time limit, Lun asked, "Can't you just reach out with ice all across the cave to find her?"

"I could. But then everything down here might not tolerate us anymore. We're already testing our luck. No need to bother beasts in their own home."

The three left just in time, and stood on top of the boulders outside. Evening began to set. Neither Rollan or Taran were sure what to do, but Lun didn't miss a beat, saying with command, "Alright, let's get another torch. Rollan, I assume you can do this, build a ice pavilion on top of the clearing, on stilts, so Taran can monitor everything for us in case Abeke leaves the caves by herself. In the meantime you'll come with me to help make another torch."

Rollan obeyed, creating a pagoda on thin spires and stilts embellished with frosty flowers and vines. Taran climbed iced stairs to the lookout tower and assured them he could do it. If he saw Abeke leave the caves, he'd be the first to notice.

Lun resisted the impulse to interrogate Rollan right away, and said, "For more torches, we'll need some moist wood. Cane, or reeds, or wet bark. I can rip my clothes to add that to the end.

But then... Rollan, is there anything flammable you know of we can dip the cloth-wrapped tip of the torch in? Pitch, grease, oil, animal fat, some tree saps, know anything?"

"Sure." he said. "There's a tree nearby that flaming pigs love, full of volatile nectar and sap. We can use that."

"Excellent, let's go." He strode forward, and took it for granted that Rollan would follow.

But Rollan took the lead, in order to show where they could find the sap. On the way there, Lun said, "You islanders know how to make torches, I presume. You didn't think to grab one when you left home?"

"To be fair, I was in a rush."

"Sounds like you're often just as impulsive as your sister then. But never mind that. That sorcery back there, the ice you conjured, how did you do it? All you mentioned was something 'bout a friend. Suka."

"As someone from the badlands, I suppose you wouldn't know. These medals of ours allow friends to communicate and share power between each other. In cases of emergencies, medals allow friends to reach across time and space to help each other. A medal represents the bond between two beings, either a human and beast or beast and beast."

"I understand. So your friend, Suka, is a beast that lends you this power. Can two humans share a medal?"

"No."

"Why not?" said Lun right away, quick to question.

"Some sages have theorized this is because humans migrated in the past to the Island, but no one is sure."

"The idea being that this ability to make medals is tied to the Island."

"Yes."

The two arrived at the right tree. Red-backed lizards and orange squirrels scattered at their arrival. Lun was about to start chipping into the wood, when Rollan asked, "Will one of these branches above us work?"

"Yes, but make sure it's hard to burn. One with moss on it would work well."

"Good." He held a hand to stop Lun from digging for the sap. A blade of ice grew in Rollan's hand. With permission he severed one of Lun's sleeves. While he did that, a tooth of ice grew on the ground and jutted into the trees. A large moss-laden branch fell.

Rollan caught it and wrapped the cloth around the tip, and tied it with an ice brace. Rollan swelled with power, growing into something more wolf-like. Streaks of his hair turned white. The blade in his hand expanded into a spear. With it, he tore open the bark. He doused the torch tip in the bloody-orange sap that bled out.

Lun had stood aside and watched all this, noting to himself yet again to learn everything he could about this magic later. Despite himself, he said, "Even if fire doesn't burn ice all that fast, woul-"

"No," said Rollan, "It's fine. Once we light the torch, I'll carry it and refreeze the tying brace as many times as needed. Now, let's go get Abeke."

* * *

In the forest, with darkness shrouding the bramble and no star able to reach past the canopy, Abeke followed Gong out of the caves and up into a tree. Gong had noticed Taran keeping a lookout and Lun with Rollan searching the caves. Gong had left the underground through a secret entrance far from the clearing, and hadn't mentioned the humans to Abeke. He'd thought them just more men on a fool's hunt.

Despite the twilight outside, he felt where everything was. Abeke stumbled to catch up. Now the two stood at the base of a tree so high neither could sense the top, branches and leaves scattering the way up, pitch-black night soon approaching.

Can you draw on me? I am curious to see it happen.

Abeke felt confident she could do it, since she'd seen Rollan pull on Suka's power dozens of times. She clenched her muscles, imagining herself growing bigger and stronger, perhaps with shiny armor.

After a minute standing like that, she conceded that her skin did not feel any harder or shinier. Gong felt he should give a tip, then decided not to. A pulse of pride emanated from Abeke. So he kept quiet.

The girl sighed, knowing the approach hadn't worked. Her mind wandered, hesitating at the solution. She remembered everything Rollan had told her, and the legend of the Chimera and Pygmy. *Please,* she asked in her mind, *I need help, and I'm not strong enough on my own.*

Though Gong heard, he didn't need to repeat the answer. He'd given the answer when they had exchanged medals.

Abeke grew a bit taller, her limbs elongating and hands and feet changing to thin stems, skin shifting to a shiny carapace like Gong's. She couldn't see her face, but wouldn't have minded her now mantis-like head missing hair. The transformation didn't completely turn her into a mantis. She wasn't as big a Gong, nor had as many legs. Nevertheless, it filled her with pride.

Good. Now, let's see how you shape up. A competitive glint flashed across Gong's eyes. The mantis, almost before Abeke realized it, had climbed dozens of feet. Gong didn't go farther, looking down and waiting to see how Abeke fared.

Ten feet high, the lowest branch taunted Abeke. She crouched in preparation for a jump, thinking she might reach it. She sprang, rocketing up and knocking her head against the branch. She twisted inelegantly in the air and floundered to the ground. She spun in disorientation, confused but not hurt.

We're durable, but not invincible.

Yeah, well, I just started, replied Abeke.

I know.

Abeke lay down again, then stood up again before realizing Gong had felt her feelings and responded. She looked up, and he looked back. Waiting.

The girl smiled, then jumped with much less force. She caught the branch and hauled herself up. Though the jump pleased her, she checked up and saw that there was still a ways to go, and they'd just started.

In a risky move, desperate to go faster, she jumped high and forward, then kicked off a tree limb to land on an arm that had originally been above her head. To stop her momentum from the double jump taking her dozens of feet up and away, she scraped her foreleg across the tree. The blue blade sprung from her arm to help. And with a wave of her arm, the blade vanished.

Now you're getting it. A couple feet separated Gong and Abeke now. *Keep up.* Gong sprinted off into the treescapes, heading farther and higher. Though he moved quickly, out of consideration for Abeke, he didn't sprint.

Abeke laughed, then leaped. She didn't slow down, and

now every branch dotting the trees turned into another place to reach. The two flew so fast even the wind buffeted them, surprised at something new bounding around.

Though Abeke hadn't thought on it, she chose many of the same trees as Gong, avoiding places that would otherwise bother the inhabitants. In one tree, dark red fire ants paused a battle they were having with wasps to watch the two pass by. A couple wasps snarled at the memory of fleeing their hive because of Gong. Those wasps were sneak attacked by the fire ants, eager to resume the fight and press their advantage.

On another tree Abeke passed, butterflies flapped their wings lazily under the cover of large flowers, spreading toxins to deter any who'd harm their tree. Abeke sensed the butterflies without seeing them, and chose a less venomous area to pass through.

Abeke stepped on another tree that happened to be home to fire ants too, and as they weren't on alert she stepped there before dashing off to safety. The ants rushed the area, alert for what might've been a raid by a hungry monkey with red cheeks. When the fire ants saw the girl far in the distance, they slowly relaxed and went back to their stations, only for a hungry monkey with red cheeks to swoop in and stuff handfuls of the little guys into his mouth before laughing and swinging away. The ants gathered again, frothing at the successful raid. Though their saliva fell on the tree and combusted, the tree had learned enough from evolution and living with the fire ants to develop an immunity by now.

By now, the two joyriders had climbed almost to the top of the forest. Ahead, Gong passed through the canopy. Abeke raced for it too, jumping with all her might. As she flailed in the open air, the light of the purple and black sky shone down, glinting off their shiny skin and illuminating the brilliant foliage of the treetops.

Abeke twisted around to get her footing, before she was caught by Gong. He set her down to sit on a net of twigs and leaves. The two didn't speak for a bit while Abeke caught her breath, but both drank in the night of colors and life.

I've never been allowed to see the night sky before alone, she said. *Rollan always had to be with me, or someone else to ensure I didn't get in trouble or fall.*

You'll see it alone one day. I know it.

It's incredible, being able to be strong enough to do whatever you want.

Gong didn't respond, instead thinking over what he wanted to say.

What is it? asked Abeke.

Near here is the territory of some bats I fight sometimes, since they want to eat me. I was thinking, maybe not today, maybe when you're ready, but if you'd like to fight them. As practice, since I assume you don't know how to fight.

Fight? But... I don't want to fight.

No? You said you wanted to be strong.

But that doesn't have to mean violence. Like, strength to do what I want and to help others.

Hm. And say... He sprouted a blade from his foreleg, then swung it. It was a centimeter from Abeke's throat, and he'd killed the momentum in a second. Gong said, *What if you're attacked? Will you attack back?*

I'll try to resolve it with words.

And what if you can't? What if your enemy is violent, or mad, or selfish, or personally wants your head. Nothing you could say could persuade them to stop. Would you fight then?

I–

And you want to help others. What if helping involves killing those who would harm your others? Then...

By this point Abeke had reverted back to being human and Gong had retracted his foreleg. Though the mantis didn't know what tears and sniffling meant, he understood her feelings. *I'm sorry. I overstepped.*

No, it's.... I. She cried a bit more and Gong sat near, projecting repentance.

You don't have to be sorry. You weren't being mean, it's just... I don't want things to go that bad. Can't I just live and be nice and let other people be nice to me? Why do things have to turn, maybe not violent, but into a fight.

Gong observed the small figure, then peered into the night and his memories. *I don't know about avoiding fights. Or about how kind life will be to you, if it'll force your hand or not.* Gong tried to reach for something profound to say. *I just don't know. But, I do know I am your friend. If you are overwhelmed or in trouble, call me, and I will defend you to death.*

Th- Abeke interrupted herself with a sniffle, and wiped her reddish eyes. *That's nice. Thank you. And if you're ever in trouble, summon me. Even if it's a fight you're having trouble with and you're in danger.*

I thought you didn't want to fight.

I don't. But maybe I can solve the situation in some way you didn't think of.

The two sat that way for a while, neither unable to think of anything more to say. Gong tensed, sensing something. A few seconds later, Abeke felt it too—there was someone traveling upward. *It's fine, I know him.*

Branches rustled and twigs snapped as two large white claws swung from under the canopy. Rollan emerged, standing on a platform of ice, spitting leaves and flowers out of his mouth and brushing his fur. He swung around to face them.

Hey Rollan. After a moment, Abeke realized he could only feel the greeting but didn't receive any message more complex than that. "Rollan, meet Gong. Gong, Rollan."

"Oh." Rollan straightened his shock and reverted to human form. Despite his desire to drag Abeke back, he calmed down. "Hello, Gong. It's an honor to meet you."

Likewise, said Gong, though the mantis could only sense the basic emotions of Rollan.

"I'm sorry to interrupt, but Abeke left suddenly from our home, and everyone back there quite misses her. Mind if I take her back?"

Gong waved his foreleg, showing his acceptance. He looked at Abeke.

"We'll talk again," said Abeke.

Satisfied, Gong crept back under the canopy.

Abeke and Rollan looked at each other for a moment, unsure what to do.

"So..." tried Abeke, "How much trouble am I in?"

Rollan's face twitched. He walked closer. "A lot." With his big arms, he hugged her. "But I'm glad you're safe. And..." He observed the medal Abeke now wore on her necklace.

She smiled proudly. "Gong is a great friend. Maybe I can even decorate my necklace more. It'll be good practice, since you never let me decorate yours."

"What can I say," he chuckled, "I like a simple look."

"Say, how'd you find me up here anyway?"

"Me and the guys have been looking for hours for you. We might've kept around the caves for longer, but a monkey with red cheeks gave us a tip on where you are. Seemed he wanted

88

to give you payback for help with a hunt, or something."

"I think I know him. Say, does my success and safety mean I'm not in trouble?"

Rollan laughed and slung an arm around Abeke, and the two walked across ice under the starlight. "Nah."

10

Worth a Shot

Rollan and Abeke found the duo again back at the ground. Abeke, having been told what they'd done by Rollan, said, "Thanks for helping Rollan to find me, though you failed."

"Abeke." said Rollan.

"It's fine," said Taran, "She's not being rude, just truthful. In any case, we were glad to help."

With the direction of the two Islanders, the four arrived at the village before midnight. The group passed a icey barricade on the way there, on the icy ramps suspended in midair. Rollan waved and took it down. Abeke looked back at the wreckage, and asked, "Why was there...?"

Rollan, not meeting her eyes, said, "A barricade to stop you from doing something impulsive, like running away. It didn't work."

Other than that, they arrived soon at the village. Abeke, ignoring the awe of the foreigners, asked, "Now what?"

Rollan didn't respond, too tired. "I'm taking a nap. Abeke, maybe give these two a tour and keep them out of trouble." He shuffled off and left the three to themselves. He turned back a moment, and said, "Lun, Taran, tomorrow we'll speak about the whole..." He waved his hand vaguely, "Legal issue of you being here at all. But know, I'll treat you fair. You deserve that much."

"Thank you," said Taran as Rollan left.

"So..." Abeke, now in the position of hostess, turned around while she tried to decide where to start.

"What's that pillar?" asked Lun. His eyes had scanned the village, but most of it lay on the intricate totem spiraling to the canopy above, with the spiral staircase around it. On it had been carved designs of every animal you can think of and many more.

"That's just the monument to the Chimera. The sundial's at the top, if that strikes your interest."

Taran, having stood to a side by this point, thought of Lun's ignorance of the myth. "Abeke, perhaps you could explain the story of the Chimera to Lun."

"Oh, sure." She glanced at the totem, then at Lun. "Well, long ag—"

"Abeke!" The shout ran through the village where most were still asleep. An old woman strided to the group, stopped to nod in greeting to Lun and Taran, then approached Abeke.

"Hello mama, why are you awake s—" Her sentence was cut off as her mama grabbed her ear.

"Before I hear your excuses, introduce me to your friends."

"Oh, well," Abeke grimaced a bit with the ear grab. "Mama, these are Taran and Lunate, mostly called Lun. Taran, Lun, this is my mama, Maya."

"A pleasure." said Taran.

"Likewise." said Maya. "Abeke. For you, you are goi—"

"But," tried to argue Abeke, "Aren't you glad I'm safe?"

Her mama's grip didn't loosen. "I wouldn't have to be glad you're safe, if you hadn't run off. You are spending the entire day inside."

"But it's not day yet." This failed to convince Maya. "No, wai—"

"That's final." And with that, Maya pulled Abeke away to their house.

Taran and Lun were left standing in place, now with freedom to spare.

"That's it?" said Lun, with a small pout. "She just has to stay inside a house? My mama didn't season my food for a week if I misbehaved."

"If she's the type of person who knows the wilderness so well that she's confident about her safety," said Taran, "Then she's the type of person who doesn't like being inside."

"Weh. In any case, I saw her transformation when those two picked us up. Can't she just break out of her house?"

Taran laughed out loud, the loudest thing in the village at this dark hour. "Lunate, the authority of a parent is a powerful thing. Even when I became an adult, my mother's orders were all-powerful. Even if we grow and become stronger than them, parents can still seem as strong and unflinching as gods. Anyway, let's explore a bit while we can. I have a feeling Rollan will call a meeting for us soon."

* * *

Taran and Lun walked throughout the village. They crept through the underbelly, strolled the main plaza, and climbed the balconies. The two just stood and rested there for a while, on a lookout post above the village with low-lying branches scraping their heads. The branches shook sometimes, as if something rested on it.

Both travelers had done much in the past day. Neither wanted to sleep. Taran counted the dice and toys he'd brought, checking nothing had fallen out of his pack. Lun wrote in his journal with quick, elegant strokes. Neither noticed the old bruises anymore.

Another being did notice. A boy, Beni, drooped from the branches inches from the two's heads, and said, "Hey."

Taran turned, composed. Lun fumbled with his journal which fell into the village below. He screeched and ran down the stairs to get it, almost slipping on the way.

"Oh," said Beni, "Sorry, I didn't think you'd be so scared."

"It's fine, son. Lun's nerves are just on edge." Taran helped the boy lower from the branch and set him on the balcony. A pomegranate fell from Beni's shirt, which he scooped back up. "As for me, after everything that's happened the past day to get here, I think I'm done being surprised." Then Taran got to thinking, and smiled. "Boy, what's your name?"

"Beni. Sir, you won't tell on me, will you? I'm not really supposed to be out this late. Or out of the village, for that matter. I mean, I'm worried for Abeke, but Rollan didn't have to barricade the village for it."

"Well, I won't tell on you. I'm Taran, a visitor. Rollan escorted me here with the frantic man below, and we picked up Abeke on the way."

"That's great! That Abeke is back, I mean. It's good you're here too, I guess. Your travels hurt?"

Taran, in mock surprise, flexed one of his scratched arms. "Perhaps."

"Is Rend asleep, then?"

"Who?"

"Rend." Beni made him sound like someone everyone knew. "Why hasn't he healed you yet?"

"Son, I'm a visitor. Rollan and Abeke didn't get a chance to tell us much of town till they left. Who's Rend?"

From far below, Lun shouted, "Found it!"

Beni ignored the interruption and said, "He's a super important beast that lives with us, in the village. He should fix you up. Um, if you ask nicely. His is the biggest wooden house in the main plaza, near the totem pole. Well then," the boy resecured all the fruit he'd snatched in his clothes, then left, saying, "Nice to meet you."

"Likewise."

Lun stomped up the stairs, grumbling and clutching his journal. "Where's that brat?"

"Gone." Taran briefed him on what Beni had said, then the two followed his directions and headed to the house of a beast.

The duo observed Rend's home, a three story building and the largest in the village. They stepped inside to find a vast space that filled the house with a few chairs and several huge tables. Pickled jars lined shelves along the walls, along with other knickknacks. A monkey that was walking around inside. He turned to eye the duo curiously.

"Hello," said Taran.

Lun, still a bit irritated from Beni, wasn't as nice. "There's nobody here. It's just a stupid monkey. What, is he going to heal us?"

The monkey's expression didn't change, but the expression of the mouth on the monkey's cheek did. It spoke, much to Lun's pronounced horror and Taran's tampered surprise, "You know…" drawled Rend, "this guy, whoever he is, I think I hate him already. I'm Rend, wise guys."

Lun said, "A monk–"

"No, she's someone different." Alouette, the monkey and Rend's host, chittered and didn't care much. "Fine," said Rend, "Just drop me off near them, since they're hurt."

The monkey approached Taran and Lun and spit Rend out onto a table, where he wriggled for a bit. Imagine a slim long maggot with wires and metal intertwined in it. That's what Rend looked like. He turned, as much as you can turn without a head, toward the duo.

Taran felt, not heard, the voice in his mind, *Mosquito bites but nothing more serious. Alright, hold me near your face. Start with the scared young guy, he looks like he'll suffer more.*

Lun hesitated, not bothering to question how the two were able to communicate.

Now exasperated, Rend said to Lun, *I'm not going to your brainstem, not that you'll know what that is. I'm just going to touch your skin and heal you. I'll go inside for a moment, but that's just to mak— Never mind, you're too stupid to understand and not calming down.*

Taran decided to take the plunge and hold his hand near Rend. Rend jumped on and slipped under Taran's skin as smoothly as a swan into water. Taran prepared to feel revolted, but just felt Rend as a wave inside him, picking him inside out and then jumping out back onto the table after a minute.

Taran, for his part felt refreshed and all the welts from the mosquitoes were gone. Rend's attention was on something else, though.

That's that. I also extended your lifespan by ten years, I'd guess. Unclogged some arteries and adjusted your eyes. Almost like you spent a lot of time somewhere very bright.

"Well, tundras, where I come from, can have large sunglares because of all the reflective ice an—"

Yeah yeah. More importantly, how many people have you two been in contact with since you got here? Humans, specifically.

Lun, deciding to overcome his fear and replace it with annoyed determination, answered. He wouldn't let this little parasite scare him. "We've seen Rollan, Abeke, a kid named Beni, Maya, and your rude self."

Oh, the chick speaks. So the entire village will have to be immunized against your chicken pox. Thanks a lot, you jerks.

"Hm." Lun was frustrated at the little beast's stubborn refusal to be undermined. "Just heal me already."

Rend did so, much to Lun's displeasure. Then he leaped out. *Alright, you're free to go, though make sure to spread the message that I want to see everybody in the village.*

"Rend," said Taran. "Thank you for healing us. And for agreeing to immunize the village. What we heard was true, you are a essential part of the village."

Rend swelled in pride while he crawled back to Alouette. *Why, your welcome.* Rend addressed Lun when he said, *Hear that you worthless piece of trash? Learn to respect your elders.*

* * *

By noon Rollan had woken up and called a meeting. Rollan led them to his house. The furniture, from benches to chairs to tables to a bed, were intricate intertwining ice sculptures. They had cushions of wooden fiber on top. During Rollan's absence, everything had half-melted, leaving puddles soaking into the wooden floor. Rollan had refrozen the furniture, but the puddles remained. Ice sculptures also littered the windowsills and space, crude recreations of people and beasts from afar. The informal meeting started in the living room.

"You have a lot of questions." Rollan said.

"First of all," said Taran, "who's your leader? The village has a head, I imagine."

"Fair enough, but why don't you assume I'm the leader?" Rollan asked.

"You seem great and all, but you're young and from what I've heard not the best planner," Taran replied.

The comment didn't bother Rollan. He'd learned that the time Kawm almost slid off the edge of the village, right after Rollan had erected the ice. "Our leader is Rend, who's a beast and not very sociable. So I'm here instead. I assume you've met Rend, since you're uninjured."

Lun nodded his head, trying not to grimace. "Rend."

"Yeah, Rend is..." Rollan trailed off, realizing what Lun was asking why him, and not who he was. "Okay, it may seem strange that Rend is the village chief, but there's a good reason for it. See, he can heal and change anything he touches. He can fix broken limbs, heal sicknesses, and is just very valuable in the web of life of the forest. So he made a deal with us a couple years ago. We protect and shelter him, and in exchange beasts all across the forest refrain from harming humans, so that they can be healed by Rend. At least, if they can reach him before dying."

Taran said, "All the beasts in the forest agreed to this?"

"Eh, no. Many would just like to eat Rend instead. Others just ignore the treaty and bother humans anyway. In any case, here we are protecting him. But we're getting sidetracked. What else did you want to ask?"

"Are we prisoners here?" asked Lun. "What with the isolation and all, are we trapped? Second, we bring propositions to you from the outside world. And also, why is the isolation a thing anyway?"

"I'd like to know too." said Taran. "I've waited decades to learn."

Rollan blinked and chuckled a bit. "Lots of questions, where to start... The beginning would be a good place. The people on the Island have lived here forever, or for millennia, depending on who you ask. We have a pretty good thing going here, navigating the web of relationships in each quarter of the Island. Arrangements like that let us thrive. But we Islanders are also rather fond of keeping things that way. Few have traveled outside the Ring, and certainly no friends from the badlands. I mean, the far outside. Though our boats are hardly good for travel outside the Ring anyway. And while there's the occasional traveler to the Ring, we prefer to keep ourselves strong here on the Island. If we shared our secrets and others tried coming here to make friends and return to their homeland, it could upset the balance of power outside the Island. And who knows? If a outside nation built an empire or some such, it could very well turn its attention to us." He paused a moment, choosing his words, before continuing, "This all escalated when a few decades ago, before my birth, one powerful human sailed off into the wide world. Ambitious deserter, he was. We decided to close off, even to the Ring. With all that said, what's your proposition?"

Lunate puffed up. "I am an envoy of the great nation Astria, past the Ring. We are great seafarers who have built marvelous ports an—"

"Please, just skip to the point."

"We want to establish trade between Astria and the Island. An alliance. It'd be beneficial for both of us. We could enrich each other through the exchange of technology, information, and goods. I can give the final details later, since I'm still surveying your culture."

Rollan's eyes flicked away, wanting a chance to think, but first he looked at Taran. "And what do you want?"

"To secure the Ring's prosperity." said Taran, but Rollan could see that wasn't it. Thoughts were swirling in Taran's head that didn't settle. He'd have to ask Rollan about it again later. "To make sure we don't get the short end of the stick again. But Rollan, are you sympathetic to our cause? And even if you think the Island should reopen, well... That's not your call to make, I take it."

"What I think? Everything you've suggested so far goes against much of what I've been taught in life. You're proposing the Island not just open its borders, but engage with the outside. If things were just a bit different, I'd just harden my heart and send you two off in the shabbiest boat I could find."

He paused here. Lun almost said something, but Taran laid a gentle hand on the Crusader to tell him to stop.

Rollan continued, "But, I trust my senses. You seem good people. You helped us out. That counts for something. Let me rustle my contacts, and see what I can do. This crazy idea of yours... It could be worth a shot. Off you go, I've work to do."

And off they went.

11

High Kicks

The duo had split up. Taran wandered, lost in his thoughts all alone. He supposed he should go greet somebody, but he wanted a bit of time to think.

"Hey." Two kids approached him, Beni and a girl. Beni, Taran noticed now in the light of afternoon, had scraped knees and arms, as if he often went climbing. The girl had her hair heavily braided, and both observed Taran with excitement. "You're Taran?" the girl asked.

"Yes. Nice to see you again, little boy who I have never met." He smiled, a reflex when children were near him. Smiles tended to put people at ease. "What are your names?"

"No need to pretend Taran," said the girl. "I know you met Beni last night. This clutz is my bro. Say, he said he surprised you, but tell me, he fell off a branch, didn't he?"

"Kawm, don't get us distracted," Beni scolded. "Focus, before we have to help with chores."

"Right." she said. But she did notice Taran mouth a silent answer to her question, *maybe*. She giggled and said, "Abeke told us you're from outside the Island. You don't seem bad though, and Abeke put in a good word for you. Said you knew nothing about this place and wouldn't survive a day—"

"Ouch," Taran said in good nature.

"But that you're okay. So, since you come from so far away, can you teach us new games?"

"And then," said Beni, "we'll practice all day without Abeke and get an advantage over her while she's grounded. Hah."

Kawm shoved him, and Beni stopped smiling.

"Okay, we can give her time to practice first," he conceded. "So, any games you want to teach us?"

"Of course. But…" Taran hesitated.

"What is it?" asked Kawm.

"Well, the games might be too exciting for you. They're difficult games that take time to master. So maybe I should start with kid games, better for babies…" He trailed off, knowing from the blaze in their eyes that he'd created enough suspense. "Alright, I'll teach some games. You're big, you can probably do them." Taran sorted through his memory, searching and choosing and discarding games he knew. No gambling or small games, something with activity and flair. "Do you have a big blanket or cloth here? Big enough to hold a person in it."

"I don't." said Kawm. "Beni, do you know where we can get one?"

"No. What's your idea?" asked the curious boy.

"Since where I live is filled with tundras… You know what tundras are, right?"

"Yeah," said Kawm. "Rollan told us about them when he visited that quarter of the Island and met Suka. Oh! Do you mean blanket toss? Rollan mentioned it."

"So you do know about it. Beni, do you know what it is?"

"I always, um, asked Rollan to make me ice sculptures for me instead of telling me about his travels."

Taran knew he could explain the game, but let Kawm do it instead, knowing she'd enjoy that. Kawm said, "It's when a group of people hold the edges of a blanket so it's in the air, with a person in the middle on top of the blanket. Then, the group, like... not throw it." She faltered a bit as she tried to explain it in words. "The group fling the blanket up so the person in it is thrown into the air, then the group use the blanket to catch the person when they fall. Rollan said it helps people see farther, since they can see far in all directions."

"Well," said Taran, "until someone can make a blanket like that for you, I know an even harder game you can play. And while it needs something extra to play too, I think I know who can help build it."

That led to the three combing the village to find Rollan while villagers looked on in amusement to see what plan would be hatched now by those kids. Lun, in the meantime, stood to the side, scribbling in his notebook and sighing at the antics every now and then.

Beni found Rollan on top of a roof shuffling and reading through letters, though that ended when he was pulled along to a bright square in the village. Confused, he listened to Taran's detailed explanation and nodded along. Rollan planned the thing in his head and chose a spot far from an edge or house, and made sure the floor was not smooth ice so that nobody's foot would slip.

Rollan held his hands out and concentrated. A pole rose from the ground, ten feet tall, followed by a stick stretching to one side with another more fragile stick attached to it reaching down. At the end of that was a soft shell in the shape of a ball, suspended four feet above the ground.

Taran nodded in approval and thanked Rollan. "Thanks, buddy. You can join to play too."

"Thanks for the offer, but I'm busy right now. Got stuff to do. But..." Rollan looked at the structure and a glint came into his eyes. "This is going to be fun, and Abeke is going to love this too. It's a good idea with bringing blanket toss around here. Though I imagine Lun wanted more cross-cultural exchange than just gam—"

"Alright," said Beni, "Move aside, Rollan, you're distracting him."

Rollan shuffled off.

"What's this game?" Beni asked.

"High kick. Simple. Just kick the ball. Usually we have a pole and a ball on a string, but this is nice to throw together in a pinch. The height is also lowered to make it easier at first."

"Yeah, well, you'll see." said Kawm.

By now a couple adults had gathered to watch out of curiosity. A few wondered if they could get a turn later. Beni started out, eyeing the ball as the others gave him space. As a kid, the ball taunted him at eye-level. In his mind, the ball had already shattered before his astounding agility.

To start, he stood and kicked with one leg. It didn't go anywhere near the ball's height. At this point, Taran realized Beni had no idea how to do it. Then Beni, eager to not be pushed aside by Kawm, tried kicking sideways and almost toppled over.

When Taran saw the boy wanted to try jumping with both feet, he stopped him there. "Okay, we don't want anyone to get hurt."

"So," said Kawm, "how do you do it?" Her words also spoke for the curious onlookers gathering who were watching eagerly by now.

If you want to understand the challenge behind a high kick, then try it for yourself dear reader. Stand up if you can and see a ball at your eye-level. How would you try kicking it? After a few clumsy attempts to kick that height, you'll know the difficulty. Unless you're already a high-kick expert.

Taran held both arms out and pushed back the others. For Taran, the height was easy, and he wondered how soon he should tell the kids the ball could be set a couple feet above their heads. Even old, Taran could do this. He lowered himself on the floor, holding himself up with his hands and feet, stomach facing up. Then he sprung into the air, swinging his legs over his head to get momentum and exploding in something between a somersault and kick. Since the ball was so low, he hit it with more than enough force. It shattered and scattered ice across the crowd and himself. Taran landed back in his starting position easily. Though he didn't have as much experience kicking these days, he still had it.

"Alright then," he said, "Someone get Rollan to form another ball. If anyone has questions, I'm always up for answers." He bowed for the clapping crowd and left. Though he sensed several of them wanted to talk to him and get to know him better, Taran wanted a bit of time to think alone again.

His wanderings took him to a balcony constructed to overlook the village. The same one he'd met Beni on. A few flights of stairs were needed to reach it, but Taran didn't mind. Here, surrounded by leaves and branches and with a view of the forest, the sounds of the animals in the distance, branches in the wind, thoughts were all he heard. The worry that picked at his mind unacknowledged so far was this. Around his neck, a faded leather cord held two charms of great importance to him. The faded but sharp canine tooth was from Taran's first hunt, a sign of respect to the first seal he had ever killed. More than the pride of taking her life, Taran had been proud that he'd no longer been a metaphorical child. No longer weak. The other charm, a small obsidian carving of two folded hands, had been harder to obtain. And that past kept bugging Taran, with imaginings of a possible future. From everything Taran had gathered, Astria and others near it, along with the Island, were more powerful than the rest of the world. What would happen then if ships improved, and people could sail farther? Maybe Astria's current emperor might not invade other countries, but one day another would take his place without those hesitations. They'd invade and colonize others. And with better technology and magic no one else had, nobody could stop them. Except other similar colonizing countries competing for land, maybe.

Taran didn't want the world to go down that route. And so he pondered what could be done.

* * *

Some time after that, Lun strolled along toward the overlook to catch up with Taran. "Quite the game you've set up. More than one target has been built by now." The Crusader waved to the view below where adults and children gathered to compete.

Taran grinned. "You want to play? You're fit enough, and skilled enough, to master it."

"Well, uh, maybe later. It's just that we have a goal here." Lun waved his journal around a bit for emphasis. "Are you making sure to focus on what matters?"

"Yes, but it's good to relax every now and then. And I'd say I brought a bunch of fun to the village, wouldn't you?"

Lun didn't answer, instead joining in looking at the crowd below. They had gotten Rollan back, and kept him there so a long line of players could play. This lasted a while until Maya came along and broke it all up, urging people to stop ignoring their responsibilities and play when all the chores weren't done. Even though many in the crowd were adults too, they left without protest. Or at least, any protests didn't last long.

"Lunate. What are you planning to propose to Rollan and the Island?"

Lun leaned on the rail. He kept his face neutral. "All this writing, all this planning, I do it for my country. It's more than what you do, exploring and learning for the sake of it. I plan all this for Astria. And at first I thought this meant colonies in the Island and Ring, being able to extract loot and resources to Astria. Guttio and Minis, countries near my own, they've done similar projects across the world. But as for doing that here…"

Taran said, "You've abandoned that plan, I'd guess. Hard to imagine anyone seizing the Island by force." Taran grabbed Lun's shoulder, "I also know that won't discourage you. What new scheme are you planning?"

"I'm not sure yet. You'll know soon enough. Let's change the topic. Taran."

"Yes?"

"I need your advice. I'm not very good at diplomacy. And I want to talk to Rend, but I need to gain a better approach before trying again. You saw what happened last time."

Taran thought about that, then asked a question that would help solve Lun's problem, "Why do you want to talk to Rend?"

"The ice totem in the village. I climbed all the way to the top.

It's incredible, the whole thing is detailed with a skill as good as the best sculptures I've seen in Astria. Perhaps even... better. Incredible, considering how primitive these people seem. The top of the pillar even has a sundial and is above the canopy, though the place terrified me. I think some big red birds in the distance eyed me hungrily." Lun gave a little shudder before continuing, "And the sundial at the top, the floor around it is carved like a jaw with hundreds of teeth. There's just so much I want to know about the myths and culture here and the science Rend seems to know. But he's... Rend. So?"

Taran didn't have to consider his answer long. "Seems to me you two should be best friends. You're both smart, bad at communicating with others, and— might I say— arrogant. Just think of how you'd love someone to talk to you. Perhaps someone asking about what you know, appealing to your ego. I think you'd be delighted to talk."

The criticism didn't bother Lun, because he knew it was true and because it was good advice. "You know, I think that'll work. Thanks, Taran."

* * *

Lun hadn't mentioned it to Taran, but the detail on the pillar that most intrigued him was small, almost invisible, unless you spent enough time looking at the pillar. Every animal carved on the pillar, every lion and spider and frog and dozens more, didn't have a rear end— their backs fading into a mass that connected to every other animal. As if they all came from the same place, leaping out of something. Or were all the same thing, with different heads or different bodies.

Lun returned to Rend's house, searching and finding no one until a hoot from the rafters drew his attention up. He had to squint his eyes. The tall building didn't have much light inside and there weren't candles.

"Hey, kid." Rend smiled from the side of the howler's face. "Alouette, bring me down a minute, please."

As the monkey swung down, Lun was a bit miffed and kept his comment from being rude. "Maybe it's a bit hard to tell, since you're a beast, but I'm not a kid."

"I know," Rend said.

The monkey ignored the other two while they talked. Alouette sat on a table and worked on a fruit, peeling back red spikes to get at a white juicy interior.

"What do you want?" Rend asked.

"I..." Lun swiveled a bit and sat on a table too. "I wanted to talk to you. You're probably the smartest person in the village, so talking to you would be a great way to learn more about the Island."

"You've got that right." This kept Rend in a good mood, and he grew an eye on the side of Alouette's face to be able to look at Lun. The eye... It didn't seem right, like it shouldn't belong to anything. The pupil and iris were too small, the eye too big, with red veins stretching across it. A moment later, it shifted, correcting itself—the iris growing big enough to be a clear crimson.

"So, uh..." Rend said, then tried to assert himself. He wasn't used to teaching others. "What did you want to learn about?"

"First of all, the pillar in the center of the village. Does it mean something, or is it a tradition on the Island?"

"Huh. That pillar is supposed to represent everything. Do

you like hearing stories much?"

"Please, go ahead."

"Well," Rend gathered his thoughts, then pressed forward while ignoring Alouette's slurping. "Thousands of years ago, when the universe was young and the stars shone even brighter in the sky, the Chimera ruled over the world. And no one could dispute that. All who saw the Chimera surrendered without a fight. And though many creatures existed in the world, none could match their glory in any way. When they wanted a drink, they went to a lake and slurped it dry. When a mountain blocked their path, they climbed around it. Or jumped over, if they were in a rush. On a bad day, they would swipe the mountain aside. When they were hungry, their all-knowing senses scoured the world for the ingredients for a perfect meal.

"So the Chimera lived and thrived. But it did—" Rend noticed Lun raising his hand. "Yes?"

"What did they look like?"

"Good question, because nobody seems to know. Or at least, nobody agrees. I've heard mountaineers describe them as a ball with thousands of heads that could reach any direction. In the desert, they're described as a four-legged beast with hundreds of teeth. I like this region's interpretation best, that their massive size held thousands of patterns throughout their body that gave them every ability in the world. In any case, the Chimera's time didn't last forever.

"One day, all the creatures of the world felt a chill, sensing something coming and hiding in preparation. The Chimera felt the arrival too, but didn't flee. Such was their pride. A star alighted from the heavens and stood before the Chimera, wishing for battle. They agreed, and both fought. Every blow sent boulders raining across the land, swipes carved canyons across the earth. A few versions of the story even mention the world herself joining the fight. Volcanoes erupted and lightning thrashed across the sky. Earthquakes thrashed every mountain and wildfires scorched every forest.

"Despite their power, the Chimera lost, finally succumbing under the onslaught of the foreigner. Laughing at a good fight, the star left. The star seemed happier at the length and chaos of the fight, rather than that it had won. The Chimera lay injured and bleeding at the top of the world, their rivers of blood darkening the oceans.

"As they lay down and waited for death, a little human and beast approached. Even though the Chimera dwarfed them in size, making them feel like ticks crawling across a monkey's skin, they approached and began mending the Chimera, stitching and disinfecting wounds while bandaging scars with giant cloth weaved by every caterpillar and spider and worm in the world..

"The Chimera hadn't expected such kindness, but enjoyed it. After recovering— though never again the same— the Chimera began helping out where it could. Clearing a river there, opening water channels there. At the time of their death, they were much beloved the world over. And this Island, see, this place is the Chimera's grave. We're all their offspring, they are our ancestor, blessing us with the best of their powers and abilities. At least, that's how it goes."

Lun nodded, a bit unsure of what to say. "Thanks for telling me all that. But from the way you ended it, I sense you don't believe it?"

"Eh, I just haven't seen any compelling evidence. The Island is odd compared to the rest of the world, but whether that's because of the Chimera or..."

"Could there be another reason?"

"Maybe, but I wouldn't know. I know a lot, but not everything. What makes stars shine, or waves crash, or anything that makes life work at all. Whether there's something divine in all of it, or religion and stories are just a way to add spice to the world around us, I don't know."

"Yeah." Lun shifted a bit, trying to get comfortable after sitting at the hard table for a while.

"Open up the cabinets in the corner, next to the pickled vegetables," Rend said. "There'll be palm leaves you can use as a cushion. Sorry, I'm not used to guests."

"That's okay." said Lun. He went and got the leaves, creating a makeshift cushion, then sat down again and asked, "So you're the Island's best doctor?"

"That's right!" said the beast, smiling and proud. "Not even other burrowers are as good as me. I make it my mission to be the best at this."

"Don't you have any students?"

"Well... other burrowers think I'm a bit odd, and all the beasts and humans are discouraged that they can't root around in bodies with my finesse, so they don't see the point."

"There's so much you could teach me. I'd be willing to learn, and I know an entire," Lun fumbled with his necklace a bit, bringing the amethyst charm to light. "In my scholarship I specialized in history, but I know many doctors. They'd love to meet and talk with you."

"But you don't even know what you brought over. You know I need to immunize the village against that chicken pox you foreigners brought, right?"

"That's..." Lun frowned a bit in confusion. "What does immunize mean?"

"See what I mean. Where would I start? There's cell theory, virology. Do you even know what a white blood cell is?"

"Okay," Lun admitted. "There'd be a lot to learn. But the outside world would learn all that eventually through luck and ingenuity. Wouldn't you rather be the savior who taught it all?"

That sentence hooked Rend. "That would be interesting."

"Can I keep coming back to visit and talk with you? I would also like to share what people outside the Island have done, because we're not as primitive as you think."

"Well..." Rend conceded, surrendering to his curiosity. "Sure. I have a feeling we'll be good friends."

* * *

Rollan lay on his back in the city's underbelly. The hard floor didn't disturb his thoughts. His open eyes stared at the ceiling. He remembered the best time of his life. Anytime he said that to someone, they joked about how the best time of his life was also the most dangerous. Rollan didn't mind. That trip to the tundras had been spectacular. The white hills and wonders he'd seen always came back to him, haunting him with their out of reach beauty. The traveler had been, in his youth, to the mountains and deserts too. They were both spectacular, but now he missed them all. The way lakes between the mountains sparkled, how the sand dunes piled as high as trees, th—

"Thought I'd find you here."

He looked up to see Abeke's mother looking down. "Hey, Maya."

She sat down near Rollan and looked up at the bare ceiling.

"Nice ceiling."

"Are you after me because I'm not at work?"

"No. I just heard all the business about you receiving letters asking to just throw out Taran and Lun."

"Maya, I know you think our isolationism is a silly paranoid ditty—"

"Because it is."

"But we can't make a decision so quickly, the other regions have to give their input too."

"We, our, enough of that. Rollan, what do you want?"

"Well, everyone knows that'd it'd be best to keep the Island closed and safe, so our power isn't weakened by opening up to the re—-"

"No. I didn't ask what everyone wanted. What do you want?"

"Hm. Maya?"

"That's me."

"Is the rest of the world as beautiful as you've said it is?"

"That it is."

Rollan kept quiet for a minute, and she didn't probe him. "Then I know what I want. It'd be the greatest shame of my life to know there's a massive world out there and I can't see any of it. I'll see what I can arrange." A pillar of ice pushed him back to his feet, and he ran off before stopping and sliding. He came back and kissed Maya on the cheek. "Thanks, mama."

Maya wasn't Rollan's biological mother, but she had given him his fascination while growing up hearing her stories of travel. Taking the time to tell those adventures, Maya hadn't expected her stories' effect to be so wide-reaching. But she smiled, it was a pleasant surprise nonetheless.

12

Dawn

Abeke paced in the shadows of her house. Not much afternoon golden light entered through the windows, a shame since it had traveled a few hundred million miles to reach Abeke's window, and the girl could've used more of it. Naps weren't a habit of hers and she'd exhausted all the games she had at home. Boredom had crept in again. Beni and Kawm had visited her earlier to ask about her outing, of which they'd been excited to hear, but Abeke had encouraged them to play around and meet Taran before Maya shooed them away.

Looking at some wooden dice she'd scattered on the floor, she wondered if carving would be a good time-burner. Abeke flexed her arm, imagining the hard skin that had enveloped her the night before. Just like her first time, nothing happened. Tired of watching her friends play outside, Abeke called on her new friend, the mantis.

The call went smoothly. She held up her medal, linked to her necklace. Though the detailed rendition of Gong didn't move, the feelings and thoughts of the two managed to cross the distance and reach each other.

Gong, are you there?

Abeke? What's the matter? Are you okay?

I'm fine. But I missed you. Abeke didn't want him to think she'd only reached out because she was bored. He meant more to her than that. *Tell me about your day.*

I see. Gong pondered that a moment. *Well, today was meant to be a fine hunt, but then a swarm of bats tried to catch me. It didn't work, as you can see, but it was quite the threat. I didn't manage to even scrape any of them. If it had just been one on one... Cowards, trying to swarm me. Tell you what, if I think you can help, then I'll ask. But don't worry yourself over it.*

Don't worry about my friend almost dying?

It's just life's risks. The mantis hesitated a bit. *Besides, I'm sure you have plenty more friends.*

That doesn't mean you're any less precious. If I'd been there, I would have helped you. You get in trouble, just summon me. Alright?

Sure. Gong didn't share his thought about Abeke not being a fighter. The comment would've just made her madder. *Enough about me though. How are you?*

Trapped in my house.

Oh. That doesn't seem like something your home should do. Can't you just cut your way out? Or I can visit myself.

Okay, I'm not actually trapped. It's just a punishment from my mama for running away to meet you. She wants me to introduce you, by the way.

Sure.

Oh, and can you teach me how to carve things?

Of course, it's easy. Get your blades, then cut something. Simple.

Abeke waited a moment to see if he was joking. Then she said, *I was hoping for more specific advice.*

I don't have much experience as a teacher. This might take a while.

Abeke laughed bitterly. *It always does.*

* * *

The next day before dawn, Abeke jumped out of her window into the forest, transforming mid fall. She stuck the landing—except for some dozing blue jays who chirped at her— and after a quick apology dashed off to the sea through the skyline. There wasn't much time to spare, so she kept up a brisk pace. Brisk by beast standards that is, in that she almost flew from branch to branch until the trees shortened and the canopy came closer to the ground. Abeke arrived in time for the event, and chose a good perch on a steady branch with a view of the horizon and ocean and mangroves. A fine view for catching her breath. Dark blue streaked across the sky. Before the sun peeked over the horizon it lightened, foreshadowing the sunrise. But even from that great height, and with her borrowed senses, the Ring hid too far away to see.

Abeke swung her legs. Behind her, the rising greenscape began whispering and murmuring in relief at the end of the night's time, and in anticipation for the day.

A black and striped bird set up next to Abeke. It gave a sideways glance at Abeke and cawed, revealing jagged teeth.

"Hello," Abeke said.

The bird accepted this greeting and continued watching the horizon. Ahead, orange streaks painted the sky to herald the sun, which followed soon after, basking in its own glory. On the way, it colored the puffy mountains of clouds pink and gold.

Abeke hadn't watched the horizon like this before or with such a great view. Then again, until yesterday she hadn't had a friend who could give her the opportunity either.

"Thanks, Gong."

The girl wished she could watch this forever, but knew her responsibilities called her back. She stood up and stretched, awake and rising with the sun. With a hop, she was ready to go.

"Bye, little birdie."

The bird nodded to acknowledge her companionship, then turned back to the sun after she'd left.

* * *

Rollan had begun arranging his house early for the meeting. Mattresses were dusted and the frosty statues were rearranged. Well, Rollan called them statues, but they were little figures of ice Rollan had made as experiments or in boredom. Most depicted beasts, but a few cold copied plants dotted the win-dowsills. No human statues existed, except for a small one. It depicted a fat woman with her ice crystal hair pulled back in a bun, swathed in clothing meant for a land colder than anyone in the village had ever experienced. Except for Rollan and Taran, that is. The smallest detail on the figure was a medal hanging around her neck, though Rollan hadn't had the skill to reproduce a medal's details at that size.

Just as the expectant host opened windows to let in a breeze and fledgling light, Lun came in. "Hello Rollan."

"You know, I hoped you'd arrived first. Come in, sit around the table."

Lun took a seat around the low table, the floor cushioned by a pillow. "What did you want to know?"

"Just a bit of advice. Do you suppose that, if asked, you could design a wooden support structure to replace the ice supporting the village?"

"Is it likely Suka will die soon?" asked Lun.

"No, but... How did you even figure out why I asked?"

"Clues. You made this structure to elevate everybody above the dangers of the jungle floor. Impressive. But it's still ice, and you keep needing to chill it. It'd be a tragedy if melting platforms made houses plummet to the floor. Suka is a great friend to you. Indeed, may she live to be old and full of days. But if something unfortunate happened, and she couldn't help you anymore..." Lun trailed off, as if unsure how to continue. Rollan knew the implications. "Abeke's new ability will help with cutting wood, I imagine. And the wonders it must be like in the cold section of the Island, when constructions don't melt. What's it like, with unlimited construction material?"

"Hehe." Then Rollan folded his hands and recalled the memories. "Slides. Very big, absurdly long slides. But back to the beginning. Can you design something like that?"

"Sure, in my dreams. As much as I love architecture, I'm not an architect. But I know people who are in Astria. And considering what you're going to say today, I guess bringing them over is a serious possibility."

"That it is."

Both sat in silence for a bit, neither noticing Taran, who stood by the door and decided not to interrupt. After a bit more silence, Lun spoke up with, "It'll be something great to look forward to. I can't wait to see it."

"Neither can I. It'll be something awesome and grand and big to show off to those stuck-ups in the mountain areas, boasting about their dumb mega structures and..." Then both noticed Taran

"Come in, Taran," Rollan greeted.

Rend and Alouette swung in through a window, waving hello.

"Rend, what a surprise," said Rollan, "I thought you wouldn't want to join."

"Not much, no," Rend said as Alouette settled onto a pillow in the corner and dozed off, nudging Rend to not make much noise. "I won't participate, but it's good to keep up with, uh, local politics. Plus, Lun invited me."

"Well, we're glad to have you."

"So." said Taran, "Rollan, what did you call this meeting for?"

"I've made progress on the idea to open the Island." said Rollan. "I want to explore and see the outside world, and people should have the opportunity to do that. Still, my change of heart doesn't mean much. The other regions will have to be contacted since they all agreed to the Island's closure. But it could happen."

Lun said, "That's great to hear, and we'll support you all the way. Both the outside world and the Island will benefit tremendously. It can't be anything but good."

"Rollan," said Taran. "Will the beasts travel outside? That is, past the Ring."

"No." he said. "Even for the beasts who go the distance, the swimmers and fliers and whatnot, none ever leave."

"Why?" said Lun.

Rollan shrugged. "They always give vague answers. That they belong here or feel some attraction."

"In any case," said Lun. "The world will see a great boom."

"But will it?" asked Taran. "Mind if I tell a short story? It's about how I got this." Taran showed his obsidian charm, of two folded hands.

Rollan didn't know the point of it, but figured Taran had something to say. "Go ahead."

"As a kid, I was inspired to travel and meet a nearby tribe, the Kerms. When I arrived, I expected rude people living in caves, per tales my chief at the time spun about them. Instead the Kerms welcomed me. Most of them, anyway. Both chiefs had a rivalry and were raring to bring us to fight. But I disagreed. So I organized protests and traveled between both tribes, avoiding a fight. This charm, fashioned by the Kerms, was a gift I received. My wife even used to be from there."

"Impressive" said Lun. "But why bring it up now?"

"Well, sometimes, I wonder. What if either now departed chief had had some special ability or weapons— like weapons of magic metal, or to throw lightning, or even, just maybe, the power to create ice—he might have gone ahead with a slaughter. At this dawn of a new age, I can't help but feel that Astria and the Island would be in a very powerful position to conquer the rest of the world who don't have friends in high places. Or at least the rest of the world would be exploited. I have the feeling that if the Ring had held things Astria wanted..."

Everyone understood the implication. The Ring, weakened by disease, would've toppled over.

"Taran," said Lun, "isn't that a bit pessimistic?"

"You know what the world is like around Astria," Taran reminded him. "If any of those countries had overwhelming power, would they hesitate to colonize or conquer the others?"

Lun didn't answer. He said, "This does bring me around to my big proposal I'm going to give. Astria and this Island, I believe we should forge an exclusive alliance. Of trade, of mutual aid, and if need be, warfare. At first, arriving at the Island, I did think that force would be the way to go. But I see differently now. Cooperation would be better. Taran, I understand what you're saying about a massive power imbalance. Astria, I admit, would prosper and raise itself in this relationship above the other nations. But to think we'd abuse that power? There's rules we adhere to, things we obey. An Astrian can't just enslave others or commit atrocities without being brought to justice. It'd be immoral and illegal."

"Immoral and illegal, sure. But if it's profitable, then someone is going to do it eventually. And perhaps you think exploitation is wrong. But can we trust everyone, even future generations, to think the same as us? Will every single Islander and Astrian withhold from cruelty?"

"There is also..." Rend faltered a bit as everyone remembered he was there and turned to look at him, "Disease spreading to non-immunized people would be a great problem. Like what happened at the Ring." After a moment, it occurred to him to say, "Tragically."

"I'm confused," said Rollan. "You bring up interesting points, but are you saying we should keep the Island closed?"

"No. It's about time that this ended," Taran said. "But we will need a plan so the world doesn't turn into a frantic scramble for land and power. Or at least, an unbalanced scramble. I'm working on something though, and assume you'll give me an opportunity to present the plan."

"Sure. It'll take a while, but it's possible," Rollan agreed. "Several prominent people from across the land could come here soon, envoys of each region. Everything will be decided at that reunion."

"Great." Taran observed the room of wildly different people, whose homes were sometimes hundreds of miles apart. "Good luck to us all, then."

The group all filed out, leaving just Rollan sitting behind with Rend and Alouette. Rollan drummed his fingers on the table, outlining in his head the letter he'd send to Tenga, and Mani, and also to Dizz. Then he looked back and remembered Rend hadn't left. "Yes?" Rollan asked.

"Everyone forgot about the birdpox."

"Oh. Is that why you've been calling people in the village? Will we be fine?"

"Yes, yes. Just invite the humans from other areas and I'll immunize them. And, thinking ahead to this spreading to other regions, I have a plan. I'll just make a new virus that immunizes people. It'll probably work. Probably. Alright then, Alouette, let's go!"

Alouette flicked one eye open and looked at Rend in laziness.

Rend said, "Yes, now is the time to perform ethically dubious experiments! Great morning for it, really. But, uh, after you've had breakfast, Alouette."

Alouette grunted in satisfaction and clambered back out a window, ignoring Rollan's gestures to the door.

13

The Basket Sled

Everyone prepared ahead over the next couple days except Abeke, who spent quite a bit of time playing or working. Both of these were helped along by her new abilities, though Maya grumbled that blades wouldn't help weave faster.

The others prepared in their own way. Rollan sent and received letters while Taran and Lun rehearsed their ideas and what they'd say. On the side, Taran got to know Maya to discuss their shared cultures, while Lun pulled Rollan away from letters and pining to help with ideas of his. Most of those ideas melted and fell into the forest, but Lun insisted on their importance.

"So," Taran asked Maya once, "What happens if a cloud crosses from one area of the Island to the next. How does that border work?"

"It's abrupt, but it makes sense," she explained. "To us, at least."

"But in the rest of the world, including the Ring, nature doesn't change so suddenly. Areas sort of fade from one to the next."

"That's just your logic. Maybe it's everyone else who's

strange, and we've got it normal. To answer your question, I actually got told by Bagee a vivid description. A raincloud passed right over us and headed to the desert. At the border, where from one foot to the next it changes from lush forest to scorching desert, the raincloud just stopped. Sort of fizzled as it spread out and disappeared. That's just how it is."

"Bagee... the one who left the Island and accidentally inspired the Isolation?"

"The very one. A troublemaker, but he had a good heart." Though she didn't say it, Taran sensed Maya did wish she'd get to see her son again one day. After all, it had been decades. They had no way of knowing if he even lived.

* * *

Abeke had been strolling along, munching on a pomegranate, when Lunate invited her to his outdoors makeshift desk. On the table were two books, one closed and bound, the other open and filled with Lunate's delicate cursive script. His inkhorn was open, his quill dripped, and not a spot of ink marred Lun's hands.

"Yes?" asked Abeke.

"Good day to you too. Would you mind confirming some things for me about the Island? See, here next to my journal is the incredible The Spirit Of Adventure. I've read it ten times."

"And what's in it?"

"An incredible compendium on all known facts of the Island, published back in Astria. I'll make sure to add to it."

She picked up the book, filled with large blocks of script

explaining the glory of conquest, the virtue of exploration, and with few sketches of any landscape or setting. Abeke said, "I can't read this language."

"It's fine. Just help me out a bit."

"Hey, I thought you nobody outside the Ring had ever been to the Island. Where's this book from, then?"

"Well, there's one report centuries ago from a man, Larry the Loony, who purports to have been. Culnate based this book on a translation of Larry the Loony's account. Though I prefer the writings of Pini included here. So, help me check. Tell me, where can I find the golden gulches?"

"Don't exist. At least, I've never heard of it."

"Hm, perhaps. What about the diamond dunes."

She smiled a bit. "Nope. Pretty sure someone would have found it by now." She pointed to a random piece of the page. "What's that say?"

"It talks about the arctic apples, fruit that grant unending prosperity." Lun said, "Maybe it's a tad fantastical."

"Yes. Would you like a pomegranate?" She offered him a bite from hers. "Kawm has more, if you want your own."

The Crusader took a bite but his mood still soured. He'd enjoyed the book. He pursed his lips and threw The Spirit of Adventure deep into the forest, where it would later be set aflame by a phoenix. Lunate didn't even mind if that counted as littering.

Abeke couldn't help but feel sad for the guy. So she took him away and said, "Here, I'll show something special and real."

* * *

"Throw it." said Abeke.

Lun kept holding on to Abeke's medal and cord anyway, not believing her. The two stood at an icy ledge with a fatal drop to the forest below. "And it'll come right back?"

"Yeah. Medals have special things about them."

"Properties?"

"Yes." Abeke nodded in pride. "Nobody has ever been able to scratch or damage one. They're buried with their owner. Special things, really."

"Well, I'm trusting you on this." He threw it. They both watched as the shiny medal and cord flew out of sight. Though neither of the two saw it, a bird had scooped it up.

"So it'll..." the Crusader trailed off since Abeke already held the medal again.

"Told you." Out of instinct she brought the medal to her neck, only to realize the cord hadn't come back. Her mouth formed a straight line.

"You were saying?" joked Lun.

"I'll get it back."

"Wait, wha—"

Abeke didn't catch the rest, having swan dived into the forest. Her skin glinted as it changed on the way down, and her newfound awareness enabled her to her sense the cord in the bird's mouth as she followed her path. On the way she avoided crowded branches with bugs and orchids. The bird didn't go fast though, and alighted onto a nest with her chicks.

Abeke landed with a thud on the same branch as the nest. The bird was half Abeke's size, plump with scaly blue claws and a large folded tail that sparkled with green, gray, and red colors although it wasn't unfolded. Despite the limb shaking from Abeke's arrival, the bird didn't startle.

The human and bird acknowledged each other, having met through Rollan. Abeke stretched out a patting hand and softened her shell to greet the chicks, who chirped in response.

Why? the bird asked.

"It's just that that's my cord, you see. Sorry that you can't borrow it for your nest."

Fine. She gave it to Abeke.

"By the way, it's a very pretty nest. Sturdy."

The mother puffed up in pride.

"Don't know why, but it almost seems like..."

Abeke's thoughts ended on closer inspection of the nest. Underneath twigs and leaves and old feathers lay a sturdy structure keeping it all together. Abeke knew the structure quite well, since she'd crafted all of it. "The basket-sled. What do you know." Abeke tilted her head at the mother, then smiled and stretched. "I've got to go, but I'm happy you got some use out of it. Goodbye."

After she'd jumped away, the mother ruffled her feathers and decided what she'd like to hunt that day.

* * *

"Okay everyone," boasted Abeke to the crowd around the high kick pole. "Watch how a master does it." The sport had turned out to be quite popular, and now that Abeke had left her house, she devoted herself to relaxing a bit and showing off when chopping timber.

Taran and Rollan were part of the onlookers, along with Kawm and Beni. Rollan stuck around for repairs and getting to watch the game. Taran joined to watch too, a bit because it amused him to see flailing amateurs, but mostly to give tips and help out. No one had matched his skill yet.

"Abeke," said Kawm, "No help from Gong."

"But why?"

Abeke's friend gave a straight look. "It's not fair."

"Please?" Abeke widened her eyes, then kneeled a bit in a vain attempt for sympathy.

Beni stepped in. "Just do it. She's not your mom."

"Then why do I have to keep cleaning your mistakes?" said Kawm.

"Alright, fair enough," said Abeke. To placate her friend, she added, "Just once, then I'll play fair." She gauged the pole and ball, now a target in her mind. Along with transforming, she swung her arms back, like a bird about to take flight. She jumped and misjudged her momentum. Instead of kicking the ball, she crashed into the pole and flopped to the floor. The ball fell and shattered, but so did the pole. On top of her. The chitin receded from her skin, and she stood up with Beni and Kawm holding her arms. "I'm fine, I'm fine."

Taran started clapping, joined shortly by the rest of the onlookers.

"Hahaha, very funny." said Abeke. "Did, uh, I say just one try?"

"Yes." confirmed Kawm.

"Eh. Welp, I think I'll take a break." Abeke stomped away from the group, trailed by Taran.

"Should we say something to her?" asked Beni.

"Nah. Some time alone will do her good," said Kawm.

Taran followed Abeke as she trudged to nowhere in particular. He said, "It takes practice. It does, and thinking you'll master it right away just because you have help is…" He didn't say more. Abeke hadn't focused on him yet, instead just standing still. "What is it?"

Abeke rubbed her eyes and sighed, keeping her eyes down. "Do we matter?"

"Yes." Taran paused. "But, in what way do you mean? Where's this coming from?"

"Just that." Abeke sighed again. "Sorry, I'm not saying it good."

"Take your time."

"Well, a bunch of things are happening. Gong gets into trouble all the time, everyone's deciding what's going to happen to the Island, and with all this big stuff, I'm not a part of it. And Kawm is right. Having Gong's help isn't that much after all. There's still so much to learn and master and do. You're small, but at least you're a leader for some people."

"Skulks."

"Right. And th—"

"Yeah, I'm cutting you off here." Taran glanced back at the crowd of people playing. "Yes, we're not emperors or guys who can wave and create ice. But we matter. I have family and friends I love and support. They do the same. You have that too. We're people first, and players second. That's what I think, at least. Stop." Taran needed to say that or he felt Abeke would've started panicking. "You're a kid. Leave the grown up stuff to us."

Torn, Abeke stared at the floor with red eyes.

Taran kneeled and brought her to eye-level, tilting her chin up. "Look, there's a lot of people in the world who could use your help. That's true. But why do you need to be the one to save them? Why are you responsible for everyone's mistakes?

It'll be sad indeed when kids need to clean up after us adults. So go be selfish, why don't you?"

Abeke looked back at the crowd of players.

"Have fun. Go be a kid. When you're older you'll be one of the best. I don't doubt that. But until then, and especially then, make sure to enjoy the downtime. You owe it to yourself."

Facing him back, Abeke glanced one last time at the players, then nodded. She turned around then stopped. "Thanks, Taran."

"Anytime, kiddo."

After she'd gone back to playing and practicing with the others, Taran stood by himself for a bit, in thought. He said, "That still leaves the question, can little people affect the world in big ways?" This worried him, but he smiled against adversity. "Guess I will find out soon."

14

Secrets

It was evening when Taran and Lun had been invited to Maya's household, to eat dinner with her and Abeke. The four were halfway through a soup of diced onions, squash, and meat when Rollan walked in. He was about to start speaking but Maya hushed him, gesturing to wait for business until they were done.

So Rollan sat and waited. When the meal finished, Abeke and Lun went off to wipe off the bowls in the kitchen, near a window. Taran and Maya chatted at the table. Rollan joined and said, "The conference is in a few days. Are you ready?"

Taran nodded. "Only problem is this darn humidity. Don't know how you stand it."

Rollan said, "This is paradise compared to those cold climates. My lips almost froze off there."

"Then that's your own fault. For the Skulks, every child learns early of the fable of Pini. That fool didn't listen to his betters and didn't wear proper clothing. His lips froze and fell off." Taran shook his head sadly at the old tale, and said, "They say his mouth never could tell a straight truth after that."

"Doesn't matter," said Rollan, "The jungle has got it better.

A little sweat isn't going to stop tonight's kickball tournament. Will you go to watch? I'll be playing."

Taran nodded and smiled, "Of course. Lun mentioned earlier he'd love to go." At this point Lun had left the kitchen and was rushing to the front door. Taran asked him, "Lun, you're still going, right?"

"What? Um, no." Lun had his hand on the door. "Sorry, I think I'll be busy, I've got to go." The door almost slammed behind him on his way out.

"What manners!" said Maya.

Taran frowned in thought and said, "He isn't usually like this."

* * *

Indeed, something had happened to incite Lun so. As he'd helped clean up with Abeke, a slip of paper had glided through the window. Perhaps it had been just imagination, but Lun had thought he'd heard a crackle. Lun had wiped one hand on a cleaning cloth and grabbed the slip. He'd read it before Abeke had noticed, and had left everything to hurry outside.

The paper had been a calling card. No words were written, just a drawn symbol of two intertwined eels climbing a waterfall, who merged into a fiery dragon. The symbol of Astria and of its emperor.

This worried Lun. No one on the Island should have ever seen or known this symbol. Lun doubted even Taran knew it. So it begged a question of him. Who wanted his attention?

The Crusader ran around the village. On the edge of a platform, while he looked for anything that could be his summoner, Lun vanished. A spiral of wind and lightning had swept him away.

So quick went the stormer that Lun could not even scream. The Crusader was dumped on a thick branch of a mighty tree. A figure awaited him there, sitting in front of a hollowed hole in the tree stuffed with supplies. It worked as a temporary home, though the shelter did not seem natural. Blackened burns outlined it, as if fiery claws had carved the home straight out of the bark.

As soon as Lun got his bearing and recognized his emperor before him, he kneeled. Skapho nodded at him, and gestured at him to sit. The emperor didn't seem to mind that his pristine clothes had been dirtied.

The young stormer, with a scarred eye, subdued the winds and wrapped around another tree limb. Waiting.

The Crusader switched to the Astrian language. "Sir, I..." Lun hesitated, then strengthened in self-satisfaction. His hypothesis had been right. "So it is true. You are Bagee. You fled the Island decades ago. You became our emperor. My leader."

"Impressive." said the self-proclaimed demigod. "Just the deduction expected of a Crusader. I only ever told one person in Astria my origin." Bagee seemed almost playful as he said, "What clues did you find?"

"You've always seemed foreign, no one knew your mother-land for sure. Your 'divine' abilities match the aid beasts and humans give to each other. And, well, you are here. A beast friend of yours must have summoned you to the Island. Sir, which of your names should I use? What language?"

"Address me as you would in Astria. Ele," Skapho said this to the Stormer. "You may go. Thank you for your aid."

But the young Stormer did not go, eyeing Lun with her better eye.

"You're healed." said Lun.

Skapho said, "I met this Stormer in the area, heading to a check-up with Rend. After an offering of fish from the river, she was happy to help me get a meeting in private with you. Do you two have history?"

Lun avoided Ele's eyes. Then, steeling himself, he said, "I am sorry."

Ele did not forgive him, but she did accept the apology, and thundered away from them back to the ocean.

Turning back to his emperor, Lun asked, "I imagine a bat friend of yours has been giving you information about the Island, and that you came for the upcoming conference."

"What," the emperor said in jest, "The one that will decide the geopolitical landscape of the world? How'd you guess?"

"But, with all due respect, I have this handled."

"Then I'm sure you won't mind extra aid."

Lun just nodded. "Of course. Sir, if I may go off-topic, about your, um, divinity... Was that a lie? Did you never meet the gods of Astria after all, instead using them as an excuse for the help your friends gave you?"

Skapho wondered what he could say to Lun, about his faith. Tell the truth? Or tell a kind lie? He settled by saying, "I will let you decide for yourself. Now then, give me a detailed report of everything you've learned while on the Island. It pays to be well-informed before meetings."

"Fair enough. Maya is doing well."

"Do not talk to me about my family. Stick to our mission."

And so they did into the late dark hours of the night.

15

A Helping Hand

In the days before the grand meeting, Taran caught glimpses of Lun sketching into boards of soft ice and trailing behind Rollan trying to catch his attention. With all that, Taran wasn't surprised when Lun grabbed him on the morning of the reunion and led him to a new staircase.

The path led to the canopy, with ridged floors, floral patterns set in the ice, and a small roof supported by beams. "Impressive." said Taran.

Lun smiled like a kid who'd built a sand castle and showed it to their friends. "Just wait till you see what's at the top. Let's go." He started stomping up the stairs, looking back to see Taran following after a pause.

"It's just," said Taran, "How far is the meeting place?"

"Above the canopy."

"Uh-huh." Taran trailed his hand across the rails, where intrepid orchid vines in yellow and purple had already sprouted. "Why is it so far away?"

"It's worth it, trust me. The Luxo is a masterpiece of sculpture and architecture. Well, at least in the jungle. Probably not in the tundra."

"What is the Luxo?"

"Well, I debated naming it the Lightorium, but Luxo is better, I think. And the construction took some time. At first it was a massive tower, but that..." Lun trailed off, his eyes taking on a look of concern mixed with regret.

"Collapsed into the jungle, I take it?"

"Almost got me and Rollan killed. Not by the tower, mind you. Instead by some wasps the tower hit below."

"A shame."

"But Rollan stuck with me and we apologized, and then built the revised Luxo. Took some calculations and factors and stuff. Also realized that every floor of a building has to hold exponential weight and boy, what a thing. The walls are hollow, but it should hold." Lun glanced at Taran. "Is this too complicated for you?"

"People on the Ring have to build things too, you know."

"Right." Lun said, with a bit of dismissiveness.

Scratching rang out behind the duo, who turned to see a plump bird with blue claws and a tail fan. When Taran tilted his head, the bird did too. Taran waved hello.

In response, the bird blinked and shook its tail, which then opened all the colored eyes on the tail. Those blinked too, much to Lun's displeasure. As suddenly as she arrived, she jumped back into the forest, ready to keep sustaining the information network of the Island.

The two shrugged to each other and kept on. Leaves parted to let in the light, which battered them as they arrived at the platform in the sky.

Despite the almost-noon sun, the Luxo stood proud, a hexag-onal hall with a dome, carved with every plant and animal Lun could think of, and someone already inside. He rested, dozing in the peaceful afternoon. Lun didn't greet the resting man at the Luxo yet, instead taking in his pride and joy. "All in the presentation. What a work of art."

"It's not that good." pointed out Taran. "If Rollan doesn't come back in time, the finer details on your project will melt. And after the meeting is over, I doubt Rollan will want to get back here every other day just to keep this place cold. So enjoy this while it lasts."

"It's a better bittersweet ending than most architectural masterpieces get."

"And what's that?"

"Looting. Though..." Lun's attention focused on the entrance, where beyond a big doorway two slabs of ice that might've once been the doors were smashed against ice furniture and some blankets. "Hey!" Lun called, and the dozing man opened his eyes to look at him. "Did you do this?"

"Not like there was anything else to do." The man had the appearance of an bull. Or maybe a rhino. At the least, something that could run into things and not notice if he knocked something down. His medal was strung from a cord of metal chains, depicting a four-legged ram in the mountains.

"Not like there was anything else to do..." mused Lun. "Of course. Except for just waiting for us to arrive!"

"There weren't handles or hinges on the door. Can they even be called doors? Seemed more like blocks of ice."

Lun mumbled something about how his sketches for a door made of ice hadn't panned out. In the meantime, the resting man began observing them more closer.

Taran sensed their introduction could've been better, so he held out his hand. "You must be Mani." The duo had been briefed on all the attendees beforehand. "I'm Taran, chief of the Skulks. Lun here is the ambassador of Astria. How was your journey here?"

"Decent." Mani mood brightened a bit on remembering it, the rush of speed and power across the land had excited him. He shook Taran's hand. "Maybe it was a bit rude to rush right here instead of greeting Rollan at the village, but I'd prefer if the meeting didn't last long. Waste of time, really." He didn't say it with bile, instead like it was a matter of fact.

"The, uh," Lun said, "door was meant to keep the Luxo's interior pristine. So bugs or something couldn't get in."

Mani gave a small laugh.

Lun frowned and headed toward the Luxo. Lun's sigh of resignation drew Taran to see. Inside the Luxo were ornate walls designed with repetitive but pretty designs of vines. Columns helped with the roof, and in it's center a shattered skylight let in light. Several beasts perched and explored the round table and chairs, while above from the skylight, several animal heads poked in to check if the coast were clear, then backed out when they sensed Lun's irritation.

A lemur with bright yellow eyes chirped from the skylight. One beast bumping across the chairs was a four legged... thing. Think of a hedgehog, but purple, the size of a dog, with smaller needles and a bit slimy. That's kind of what he looked like.

"By the way," gloated Mani, "Most of them were here before I broke down your door."

"Must've broken the skylight." said Taran, as he stepped around one of the slabs of ice. Around the retired door were shards of a former chair. "It's a nice detail, Lun, putting blankets and leather on the chairs."

"Okay," said Lun, not registering Taran's comment. "This

can still be salvaged. Rollan can replace the skylight again—"

"Again?" said Taran.

"It isn't the first time. Tower, remember? And for the smashed, uh..." Taking into account the slabs, he said, "Mani, can you move the ice out?" Before Mani could object, Lun said, "Actually, Abeke can just chop these up, and then it'll be easier to move."

Taran agreed and didn't mention the fact that Abeke would arrive with everyone else to see a ruined room.

Luckily for Lunate, Abeke arrived with a small group of the other adults and kids from the village who'd wanted to attend the meeting and hear. Abeke walked close to her friends, laughing at a joke, before Lun interrupted and explained the whole thing to her. She diced and sliced while humored adults began sliding small blocks across the platform and into a pile where Lun hoped it'd melt peacefully.

"Hey." said Taran to Abeke. "Where's Maya?"

"She decided to stay behind. Something crawled into the house last night and wrecked some furniture."

"She's going to skip all this for housework?" Taran chuckled. "Meticulous, isn't she."

Even with the progress made in cleaning, Lun eyed the beasts in the Luxo. On second thought, he decided to leave them. Seemed best to respect them. But mostly, the spiny one looked painful and by this point Lun expected the lemur to shoot him with lightning from their eyes. In fact, the lemur had considered it but decided that Lun seemed silly rather than menacing.

Dizzy arrived, representing the desert tribes of the Island, who'd argued over whether to send her. The lady overlooked the proceedings of ice shoving and a few kids making contests out of it.

While Lun eyed the Luxo, Mani and Taran went to meet Dizzy. She wore a linen baggy dress in shades of red and yellow. Her height meant Taran had to tilt his head up to meet her eyes, lined in black kohl.

"Hey," said Mani, "Great to see you again."

"Likewise." She turned to Taran. "You're the foreigner, I take it. Hello."

"Hello back at you. I'm Taran, Rollan already told me your name."

She nodded. On the whole, she didn't seem much for speech. "This is the meeting place, right? It is under construction."

Mani chuckled and said, "Bit of deconstruction, really."

"So," said Taran to steer the conversation away from jeers at the amateur architect, "The desert seems like such a strange place to live in. Polar opposite of where I live, and all that."

"Why's that?"

"Abeke, a friend of mine, said the desert is so hot it seems like it's on fire all the time."

Dizzy smirked, since the desert was only sometimes some-places on fire. "She's never been there. It freezes at night."

"Well then what do you know, opposites all around."

As the work continued, with Lun supervising, Rollan came up the stairs supporting an older fat lady with her hair in a bun. Her clothes had been chosen to have folds of blue in them to reflect where she came from. Abeke, who head heard a lot of her but never met her, went to say hi. Around the woman's neck a medal dangled, with patterns of blue, black, and white. A large fat bird was depicted, upright and sleek with fiery feathers forming an emperor's crown.

With everyone attending, Lun looked over his creation and sighed at all the people who had come. While he valued public participation, he knew a sacrifice would have to be made. Heavy hearted, Lun ordered Mani to knock down a few walls so there would be enough space for everyone. A few walls turned into all the walls, leaving just the pillars for the roof. That, and some touches from Rollan, and the place had never been better.

Tenga, Taran, Rollan, Dizzy, Mani, and Lun all sat around the table, each side of the hexagonal building—by then more of a pagoda—at their back. The crowd stood.

"Rollan," said Lun, "Add some seats for the viewers."

A moment passed.

"Please." added the Crusader.

The benches were erected. Dizzy's eyes flicked between the attendees. Mani lounged. Lun was the most nervous, reviewing in his head while Tenga and Taran relaxed and waited.

Lun started, trying to appear intense by folding his hands, "One day history will remember this meeting. Schools will teach students our names. That is how important this meeting is. Keep that in mind as we go forward. Our decisions will have consequences for decades. Let's establish what we're here for."

Lun almost managed to create an atmosphere of solemnity until the lemur jumped onto the table and approached him. Nobody payed the critter any mind, but the lemur sniffed at Lun before licking his face. In vain, the Crusader tried to keep a straight face. After all, none of the historic meetings Lun had read about included the details not deemed important, such as speakers being licked by wild animals.

"If the Island opened up, resources would be traded," he continued, "but beyond that there'd be a trade of culture. Knowledge, customs, wisdom, crafts, and magic will spread from both to the other. Let's choose wisely. Any questions before we begin?"

"Shouldn't there be a representative for the beasts of the Island?" asked Taran.

"Well..." Dizzy said, "who's to say there aren't representatives already."

Everyone glanced around a bit. A few more beasts had crawled in. A small bat clenched to the roof, a frenetic frog jumped around.

Dizzy added, "They'll get word of whatever we do here, but I doubt they'll care much what we do. Their lives will continue on the same. Probably."

"Okay." said Lun, wanting to steer the conversation. "Anything else?"

Mani yawned and jabbed a finger at Taran. "Why should the Ringer get to sit with us? Let him move back and stay with the crowd."

Taran kept a straight face and kept his biting remark unsaid. "What makes you say that?"

"Everyone else here is representing powerful factions. Lun seems a bit silly, but at least he's representing a big group of people who are somewhat impressive. Even if their ships got smashed."

"Not all of them," Lun said. A bit late, he realized that wasn't flattering.

"So, why does representative of the..." Mani searched his mind a bit, trying to remember, "of a tribe over from the Ring, get to join us? From what I heard, Astria arrived and they all collapsed at once from diseases."

"Mani," Abeke tried stepping in, "that's rude, Taran's a great guy. He's a friend who's helped us out."

Mani softened a bit. Not because he was convinced, but he automatically respected Abeke much more because she had a medal, even though they didn't know each other. "I'm sure you're right, but that doesn't change the facts. Why should he be here?"

"Mani," said Taran.

Everyone watched, waiting to see if the tension'd break. Lun picked his fingers in nervousness, and while Tenga had been about to step in she sensed Taran could handle it.

"Has Rend immunized you yet?" Taran asked.

"Rend, the worm that lives here? What about him?"

"He'll see to everyone here before we go our separate ways. Otherwise more than half of everyone you know and love will die. That's diseases and luck for you. Is everyone on the Ring unlucky because we weren't born in the right place to join an empire or have magic friends? Are we weak?" The determination in his voice suggested the opposite.

"Boys," Tenga said, "that's enough." She didn't say it loudly. Still, something about the tone suggested she wouldn't appreciate snark rebuttals. "Does anyone else want to pick a fight?" Nobody dared. "Good. Lunate, take it away."

"Thank you." Lun smiled now that he held the position of power again. Now, we shall start. Rollan, create one more chair."

Rollan did not get a chance to ask why. Everyone's attention went to the stairs leading to the Luxo, where sizzling could be heard, as if water boiled. Steam began to rise out of the trees.

The Crusader stood, and said, "I now introduce the emperor of Astria, the anointed of the twins, rider of eels, known the world over as Skapho..." At this point Lun made a decision, and added, "Known here as Bagee."

So Bagee walked into the Luxo, trailed by steam, as if he'd heated the ice under him, in his fine robes.

"Greetings everyone." said Skapho. He walked to Lun's side. "I have come to aid my servant here in representing Astria."

Abeke shouted from the stands, "You jerk!"

Rollan didn't say anything, but didn't make a chair for him either. Skapho took it all in stride and stayed standing. "Understandable, but let us focus on the matter at hand."

Mani shook his head and said, "I agree with the jungle folk here. You think you get to break all traditions by leaving, abandon your family and people, and then come back decades later and think you get a warm welcome back?"

Skapho said, between clenched teeth, "Treat me with respect. Who in the world do you think I am? I'm not a kid anymore! I am the ruler of an entire country, a demigod!"

"Then act like it." said Taran. "We will continue the meeting."

Lun gave his chair to Skapho, who took it. Lun layed a hand on his shoulder, asking him to calm down. Skapho did. But still, Lun remained shocked. Never, in all his life, had he ever heard that anything could rattle or enrage Skapho.

Skapho said, "To start, someone must state why the isola-tionist policy of the Island is desired by Islanders. Dizzy." The emperor chose her because he had heard little from her yet.

Dizzy nodded and leaned forward. "Bagee, there are reasons we can pretend to have. That the outside world is dangerous, or they're all dum-dums not worth meeting, or home is where the heart is. If it's fine with everyone, and even if it's not, I'll just cut to the truth. Having supremacy and being on top is neat. If our isolation wasn't strictly enforced..." she stopped a moment to look at Rollan, who despite his conviction wilted a bit. "... then outsiders would travel inside. Islanders would travel out. Knowledge and power would flow in between. Even if beasts never left the Island, humans would. People would travel and trade, and medals would leave. Then outside factions, people we don't even know, might threaten our supremacy at the top of the world." She tilted her head and smirked. "Can't have that happening, now can we?"

"Bagee," prompted Tenga, "Now we understand how Astria benefits from all this. But what about us? I know Rollan wouldn't have called all this without something to convince us."

"A good question," said the demigod, "You see... Now's not the time."

"Pardon?"

"Seriously, now's..." Bagee paused, listening and responding to someone far away. "I have to go." He stood so fast he knocked his chair down, and before he ran off, said, "Lun, I'm trusting you with this. Don't disappoint."

He sprinted off, and before he reached the edge of the platform, sparkling stars enveloped him and summoned him to his friend's aid. So quick did he leave.

Taran didn't know whether to be relieved or surprised. "Did he just bail on us?"

None of the Islanders seemed perturbed. Dizzy said, "It happens sometimes. If a friend calls for help, we answer. Lun, go ahead and answer Tenga's question."

"Well," said the Crusader, "Perhaps we could just wait for Skapho to come back?"

"No." said Tenga. "If his friend called, then it's something serious. Bagee won't be back for a while. Continue, and answer; how could the Island benefit from this alliance?"

"Right." said Lun. "As for the knowledge and technologies Astria would share to you—as a gift and as trade—I'll describe them with enough detail so you can imagine them, but not build. For one, I'm a Crusader, not a mechanic. I can't name every gear or screw. On top of that—"

"If we built it ourselves," Mani said, "Astria would lose leverage. Although, it's very convenient for you not to have proof of the miraculous things you've made, other than some sunken ships."

"Just take my word for it, and if I don't prove it after the Island is open you're free to throw a hissy fit and kick me out. No," Lun said in response to a glint in Mani's eyes, "Not actually kick me out. Anyway, where to start?" He thought a moment before continuing.

"You still use sundials, which is embarrassing. A good way to tell time, but even with building a sundial in the middle of a desert or mountain town, it's laborious to check it. Not everyone wants to keep walking back to the town sundial or have to put one on their roof. Punctuality is a value you haven't embraced yet, but Astria has with the clock. It's a mechanical marvel that keeps exact time and shows it anywhere, with or without sunlight. The greatest cities have erected clock towers so that proper appointments can be made, and organization thrives. The only time difficulty you'd have once it's brought here is where to place it for all to see.

"For those of us here involved in farming," Lun nodded to Mani, "You still haven't figured out crop rotation. Yes, you use the dual crop rotation system, which has its benefits. With dual crop rotation, two fields are kept for planting, a different one used each year so that on off-years the resting field has time to regain its strength. However, there's a superior system you haven't discovered, using three fields instead of two. Before you try guessing, this means using two out of three fields in any given year, but also using different plants for each field. Oh, and never mind all the crops we'd introduce to each other. Wait until you learn what sugar is.

"To finish, on the topic of plants, there's also heavy ploughs. While you have normal ploughs, these just don't work as well. Heavy ploughs have more weight for better strength for ploughing the soil. On Astria, this increased weight is bearable for a single farmer through..." He didn't want to say that they just had farm animals pull it. "Clever innovations. I have thought that some medalers might be able to pull heavy ploughs. But there wouldn't be enough labor to manage all the work, and anyone, not just whoever has a medal, could manage these."

Taran spoke up, "How long is this list of inventions?"

"It's a lot. I mean, there's also blast furnaces, arches, weight distribution in architecture, gunpowder, spinning wheels for sewing, advanced metallurgy, stonework techniques, concrete... This is all Astria is offering to you. And you know what's being opened in return. Through collaboration between us, our civilizations will reach unexplored heights. The question is... what do you say? Does the Island accept?"

No one had a quick response ready. Abeke had by this point disappeared, though no one noticed because of the discussion at hand.

Mani nudged Dizzy and whispered, "Is it me, or was all that condescending?"

Dizzy didn't speak back, although she agreed.

"Unexplored heights..." Taran mused, "For all of civilization? Or just a few at the top of the world."

Lun scanned the room before lowering his voice, "You're still going to go against me?"

"Representatives of the Island," said Taran, meeting everyone's eyes, "when this treaty falls throug—"

"If," interrupted Mani. "Not when it falls through, if it happens. We haven't decided yet."

"I didn't stutter," Taran said. "The Island shut itself up for selfish reasons, to maintain its supremacy. It'll open back up for the same reasons. I'm wise enough to know that. When this happens, the Island and Astria will be the greatest forces on earth, free to do as they please. You all see a rosy future, unmatched power leading to greater heights. For these two factions, Astria and the Island, that's true. But what about the rest of the world? Who in the rest of the world could fight back such an overwhelming mighty force?"

Lun almost interrupted, about to say that the other countries weren't pushovers. Then he thought better of it, with a bit of fantasizing about using magic to beat up the other countries he saw as greedy and just overall bad.

Taran continued, "What about the Ring? What about three-fourths of the world who will be below us on the ladder of civilization. How long before they're pushed around, bullied for all they have? Nobody would be able to keep us in check."

Dizzy drew lines on the table, outlines of a wide world. "What's your alternative, if we agreed with you? Set up checks and balances? Halt progress? Close ourselves again? Because none of these seem good."

"Envoys." Taran said, the scene unfolding behind his eyes. "Educated people who travel the world and learn, not just of the people they find but also to spread technology and knowledge. Think of how much the rest of the world could advance, if we gave them the chance to."

Lun's face shifted a bit. "Taran, as..." He searched for a heartening word. "...Optimistic as that is, think of the sacrifice required for that. We'd need to train and then send off people on dangerous expeditions through foreign environments. Never mind that even in your best case scenario, these foreigners wouldn't be immune to corruption. To start with, we'd trade over materials and resources that foreign lands would need, so that's another way enterprising colonists could cheat them." This time Lun addressed the room, "Not that Astria would do that, of course."

Taran held his ground. "None of what I'm saying would be easy. But the right thing rarely is. Things probably wouldn't happen smoothly. But face it, if one hundred overpowered foreigners arrive in an undeveloped land, we can bet at least one of the hundred will decide to exploit it. More people wouldn't have to suffer because they were born in the wrong place at the wrong time."

"Taran," said Lun, "Don't take them for fools." He swept his hands across the setting, indicating the Island at large. "Understandably, the Island closed for worries of outsiders gaining strength and power and undermining this place. Now, you propose the exact opposite, and that strength and power should be handed over to the rest of the world. Absurd." With a confidence befitting a Crusader, he said, "They would never agree to it."

"That was my biggest worry." admitted the old chief. "But then I realized, this plan most matches all the virtues and values of the Island. Here, in this strange weird world, attacks and war never work for long. There's always a faster fish, a fiercer foe, a bigger bird. So everyone here values cooperation and aid. Make friends, forge alliances, share what little there is to share. I have seen this over and over again as the Island's greatest virtue." Lightly, Taran paused to finger his obsidian charm.

Then he continued, "To the point, as we saw with Bagee, that any call for help from a friend must be answered at once, with no hesitation."

Tenga considered all this, and said, "Even so, we Islanders are not so naive. Not every beast wishes to be our friend, or to listen to reason."

"I know. But do we get to make that assumption of the world? Any riches or power gained from an oppressive empire will fade next to the crime of making an enemy of the world that we live in. Cannot everyone remember a time when they almost froze to death, or grew parched in the desert, or scraped their frail hands in the mountains, and a hand was extended to them? This is what I propose now. A helping hand to the world."

Lun tapped his fingers on the table, wondering if that faith in the future could take any far. "We will vote now, me and Taran excluded, if there are no objections." None sprouted. "One vote from each representative here. If the result is a tie, we continue debating and try again."

"No," said Rollan, "The vote must be unanimous. We have to all agree. We do this now. All in favor of the Island opening and creating an alliance with Astria, along with adding following the proposed envoys plan."

Rollan raised his hand first. Tenga followed shortly after. Mani, after taking a moment, did so too. Dizzy did it too.

Four hands raised in the air. All it took to change the world.

Lun smiled, in spite of himself, although Taran had muddled Astria's plans. "Thank you everyone. For the next step, us Astrians would like the representatives to go to the Ring to sign a more formal treaty. I am not sure when Skapho will be back, but I'll try to contact him. Meeting adjourned."

Everyone stood. Taran stayed near the doorway, observing

what everyone else did as they scattered outside and chatted. About each other, what happened, and daily news. Mani stomped outside, followed by Rollan and Tenga discussing tundran power plays.

Dizzy left the door last, where Taran tapped her arm and followed her. "You don't have to tell me... But why did you agree?"

"Why?" Since she was a head taller, Taran had to tilt his head up to meet her amber eyes. "Because I've been thirsty before. Hungry. Desperate. Helped." Dizzy's mind drifted off as she focused on something Taran couldn't see and didn't know. "And now I'm powerful. The others felt the same too, I think." She brushed the medal hanging off her necklace. "Chlamy'd be proud of me for growing up enough to help."

"Chlamy sounds noble. Could I meet them one day? Perhaps I could visit the desert."

"At your age? In any case, Chlamy's dead. And... I miss her. I never take off the medal, though there's no more power she can share with me."

Taran nodded. "Perhaps I could still visit? Seems there's plenty left for me to explore."

Dizzy smiled and agreed, and the two talked the entire way back to the village. When Taran got tired halfway through the stairs, Dizzy got Mani to carry Taran all the way back, the chief on Mani's shoulders and continuing their talks all the while.

16

White Fuzz

While the people of the meeting debated, things weren't so civil elsewhere on the Island. During the event, Abeke had been paying some attention while Kawm and Beni joked around. This happened a bit after Bagee had left. Then Gong's voice rang out, inaudible to anyone else.

Hello. Is this a bad time?

Oh, hi Gong. Now... She looked out over the gazebo and frowned.

Remember what you said about calling if I needed help?

Say no more. "Sorry guys, I'm off. Just got to visit Gong."

Beni and Kawm nodded. They would've said more, but Abeke had pushed past people to reach the rim of the platform. Her armor grew in anticipation of trouble.

Alright, call me over. Sapphire stars wrapped around the girl, one glitter she was there, and the next twinkle she'd re-emerged next to Gong on the branch.

Don't panic, advised Gong.

Despite that tip, Abeke still swirled to look up and around at the swarms of bats that surrounded the two. Even though they were all perched on trees that didn't reassure the girl. Most of the bats were shorter than Abeke, but that wouldn't be any help if a fight broke out. All the bats were brown and black with green streaks and swirls across their fur. And all of them focused on Gong and Abeke, waiting for a signal to kill them.

"So it's true." Bagee stood with the bats, with an expression on his face that suggested Abeke had made the situation more complicated. Shirtless, and with two medals of a bat and fiery lizard on a necklace, the man had yellow scales with emerald and crimson stripes. His loose pants were basil green with gold leaves. He'd thrown the shift away somewhere. "Kid, did your friend tell you what's going on?"

"No…" Though she tried to focus on the human, her eyes kept darting between all the beasts around them. "But I can guess what's going on. "

They ambushed me, said Gong. *Usually I clash with a bat and run away. Being eaten isn't appealing. But for the first time, they coordinated an assault on me. That human's fault, I suspect.*

The bats radiated anger, as if to dare Gong to imply again that they weren't smart enough to organize plans.

Once I realized I was outmatched, I showed my medal to the human there, hoping to stop the fight. Now the human wants to talk with you. Please negotiate. He looked hopefully at Abeke. *Can you? Will you?*

Of course, I'll do my best. But… She looked out at the crowd of bats. Revenge is a dish best served with a meal, and the bats very much took that to heart. Most bats present had never eaten a mantis. The black and blue creatures were so difficult to catch that most got to die of old age or disease. Bats didn't usually hunt targets in swarms, since the prey caught couldn't feed all who had helped in the chase. But for revenge against an uppity mantis who had evaded all their best hunters? Abeke sensed that feeling, even if the exact words eluded her. *That revenge is best served with a meal.*

Is fighting an option? Abeke didn't have much hope, but figured asking wouldn't hurt.

Sweet, sweet, Abeke. Gong patted her with a foreleg, in a gesture meant to be assuring. *If fighting was an option, I would not have called you. You are not as strong or skilled as me.* The mantis didn't intend it to be mean. He spoke blunt and matter-of-fact. *You're strong in a different way, and smarter. I trust you.*

Okay. Okay, Abeke repeated. *I can do this.* To the person, who she hoped was the right one to focus on, she said, "Hello Bagee." She frowned, trying to be more official. " I am Abeke. And you, well, I know you already."

"I... am Skapho, emperor of Astria and a demigod."

"And also Bagee," Abeke nodded, then grimaced. "Supreme goofball of the Island. Come closer so we can talk and not stand so far apart."

"Sure." He gauged the distance and jumped, landing with a thud and not much grace to stand next to Abeke. A large bat followed him, standing behind Bagee. "This is my friend Didae." Didae nodded in acknowledgment.

Abeke put an arm around Bagee like they were siblings, and said, "If I wasn't surrounded by dozens of bats ready to kill me, I'd punch you. Not enough to hurt, but definitely what you deserve. I should've done it back at the meeting. No one would have cared, I bet."

Bagee didn't get fazed. Living as a powerful guy in Astria had well accustomed him to threats. He could, however, get confused. "You seem to have it out for me. Have we met?" he said.

"No, but we both know Maya. She's not annoyed you left the Island. I am. Leaving her without saying goodbye?" Abeke narrowed her eyes. "Now that's disrespectful. And how long have you been back?"

"Yes, well, can we not discuss this now?" Bagee brushed Abeke's arm off, trying to regain the image of an aloof leader. "Isn't the current situation more pressing?"

"Fine, but you're not escaping this."

At the apparent tension, Didae asked, *Is something wrong?*

No, said Bagee while keeping his eyes on Abeke, *We were just talking about someone we both know.*

But hasn't she said anything yet to dissuade us? Once we saw the mantis's medal, we thought his friend would take revenge. This kid is not going to win if we finish the hunt. Let's go ahead and kill the mantis.

At least give her a chance. If not, we do it. Don't worry Didae, I'm on your side. If this turns violent, I'll fight Abeke if she chooses to fight. Even if she is human like me. Abeke stood by while this exchange happened, knowing not to interrupt. Bagee turned back to Abeke. "I will translate for Didae. We're a bit impatient here, but decided to let Gong call you to negotiate. Is there anything you want to say?"

"Okay," Abeke said to herself, not having much experience with tense negotiations. For a second, she wondered if calling someone older and smarter would work. Maybe Rollan or Taran. Peering into the faces of the restless bats, she guessed that their patience would break if she did that, unable to delay satisfaction any longer. "Okay, can you not attack Gong?"

"Seriously?" said Bagee.

"He's a good friend of mine, and doesn't kill bats. So why should they want to hunt and eat him? Just stick to fruits or whatever other plants bats eat."

Bagee pursed his lips. "Kid, I—"

"Don't call me kid, we're foster siblings."

"Fine. Abeke, I'll do you a favor and not translate what you just said. I have a strong feeling that won't convince my friends. Now, do you have something worthwhile to say? Or do you surrender?"

"Well," Abeke's heart picked up the pace. "What would it take for the bats to forgive Gong and leave him in peace? Is there anything that could be done, some task maybe?"

Bagee translated.

Didae said, *The mantis could let us eat him. We might forgive him then.*

"Nothing comes to mind to Didae, no."

Another bat chimed in, saying, *What if they could do something about the fuzz?*

Didae snickered. *What's she going to do to solve that?*

Maybe it's worth a shot. Bagee said. In the meanwhile, Abeke had mentioned to Gong the gist of things so far.

Gong, fearing the worst, said, *At the very least you can escape. They won't want you.*

I'm not having any of that.

"Abeke," Bagee said.

"Yes?"

"Would you happen to know any powerful doctors?"

"What do you mean by powerful?"

"Very smart, knows how to help beasts and so forth."

"There is Rend," Abeke suggested. "You wouldn't know, he entered the village after you left and abandoned us."

"No need to rub it in. That happened before you were born anyway. Focus. Besides Rend, who I already heard of, do you know somebody?"

"No. Is there a sick bat that needs help?"

"In a manner of speaking. There's a horrible disease that goes among the bats when they hibernate in caves. Most of them call it the fuzz, it's a whitish growth on their faces that saps their strength when they should be resting. It's devastating and has killed entire colonies of bats. Perhaps, we thought, you might know a way to cure it."

"Don't be silly," said Abeke. "Rend can help you. Sure, he's a bit mean and never forgets if someone spills or breaks something of his, but he would help. You said you know him, so why not just see him?"

"Because..." Bagee gave a small cough, unsure how to phrase it. "Didae, my friend, well. Before the fuzz became a big problem, Didae's son tried to catch and eat Rend once."

Didae's son said, *Hey, I said I was sorry for that.*

"Like you said, Rend has a long memory. Plus, he wouldn't be too keen on making cave visits to see the hibernators. Abeke, if you can't help then it's time to act."

Didae, having not been translated to for a while, asked for help. Abeke waited a bit while Bagee translated.

When he turned back to her, Abeke, both desperate and wanting to help, said, "I can convince Rend. He's not a monster, and I can do it. Wouldn't that be more than worth it? Letting one prey go to save a lot of bats?"

What did she say? Didae asked. Abeke and Bagee told their friends of the exchange.

With their hearing, every bat picked up on Bagee's thoughts as he explained to his friend. Didae, for her part, wanted badly to believe the offer. But wariness kept her guard up. *Bagee, despite how great this offer is we have to be careful. What if she's lying to stall and give the mantis a chance to escape? Or even worse, what if Rend decides to trick us by pretending to agree and then killing us while we're tired. It'd be the perfect revenge. This is a big risk.*

That's true, conceded Bagee, *But take my word for this. I've met a lot of liars who would tell me the sky is neon yellow if they thought it could help them. Abeke does not seem like a liar, or devious. Do any of you sense that from her? Does anyone here think she's a conniving mastermind?*

Every beast focused on Abeke, on her confusion and nerves. However, even the most cynical and world-weary bat had to admit that Abeke did not seem much like a manipulator.

Bagee said, *Despite that, you may be right. Perhaps she's a child prodigy of deception. But I would still take the risk. It's your choice Didae. What do you want to do?*

I think... I'll do it. You know, I'm not sure why. But in the same way I trust my family to help me, I must trust her.

"Abeke," asked Bagee after receiving Didae's response. "Do you swear you can do this?"

"Well, I can't see the future. But I swear to do my best. Isn't that the best any of us can hope for?"

"Yeah," said Bagee with a hush in his voice, "I guess it is. We accept. By the end of the day, let me know what can be done. I'll come to visit you in secret."

The swarms of bats flapped away. A couple, including Didae, swerved in front of Gong, acknowledging him. Gong acknowledged them in return.

Abeke's poor heart almost gave out in relief. But before she could collapse or hug Gong, she said to Bagee, "Thank you."

"For translating? Don't mention it."

"About you coming back..." said Abeke.

158

Bagee turned away at this, and though he took a few steps away, he stopped.

Abeke added, "I guess you came back for these negotiation things, and talking to everybody on the Ring once the Island decided to open up."

"You could say that. I have a small friend at the meeting who has a gift for perception, and will report back to me."

"I know you're probably scared…"

"Me? The demigod emperor of a country who's ventured this far north? What have I to be scared of?"

"Please, just say hi to her, one last time. Maya didn't attend the meeting because something, or someone, broke her furniture last night. I guess you're at fault for that." She paused to see what he said. He didn't deny it. "You're like a chief now, right? Or a divine emperor whatever. Sounds like a big deal. But can you face who you left behind? Have some courage."

"Goodbye, Abeke. It was nice meeting you." He leapt across the trees.

Gong stepped closer, his steps so quiet they were inaudible. *Thank you.*

The girl, half his height, rested a hand on his foreleg. As good friends, no other words needed to be said between them.

17

The Demigod

The inside of Rend and Alouette's house lay dark most of the time. Like it had until Taran opened the front door, through which eager light shone across the dust in the air. Lun, Dizz, and Rend followed him inside. More light flowed in as the three humans opened windows, fluffing up the atmosphere. Then Taran arranged chairs so they could chat. Alouette had swung away to chill in the rafters, and Rend had taken up residence in Lun's arm instead.

"So," Dizzy was telling them, "the screeches were so loud they rang across the desert."

"Mani was the one screeching?" said Taran.

"Yeah. I ran outside and found Mani charging across the dunes with a horde of beasts chasing him. What a cloud of sand they threw up. After I stopped the rampage, Mani explained he'd tried to travel by just running across the sand."

Lun said, "And he didn't guess that he'd hit something while sprinting?"

"The desert does look empty, if you don't see all the hidden beasts."

"How did you stop them?" Taran asked.

"With Chlamy's help. She had a stare that paralyzed anything unfortunate enough to se—"

"Hey, is Rend here?" Abeke popped in, a few branches lining her hair but none the worse for wear after the standoff.

"Abeke," said Rend. "What do you want?"

Taran waved her in. "Welcome, Abeke. What happened earlier? You left the meeting."

She blinked. "So did everyone else."

"I mean early. What happened, are you hurt?"

"She probably is," said Rend. "Abeke never comes to visit. Not that I want the company, but you could bother to try."

Sensing that Abeke might snap back, Taran soothed, asking her, "In any case, what did you want to see Rend for?"

"I need your help."

"As always," commented Rend.

"Rend." said Lun. "Listen to her for a moment, alright? This could be serious."

Rend, said, "Yeah, you're right. Sorry Abeke, what's the trouble?"

In response, Abeke summarized the standoff, reassured everyone that she was fine, then asked Rend if he'd be willing to help cure the bats when they hibernate. She didn't mention that Bagee had been at the event. She wanted to know if Bagee would confront things himself.

"I mean," said Rend, "It does sound like they need the help. But they tried to eat me..." This stewed in him a bit, but he sensed Lun's thoughts on the matter. "Ah well, I guess I should let bygones be bygones. Though, from that squirt who tried to eat me, I'll want a full apology."

"You'll have it," reassured Abeke.

"Hm. But, I'll need to travel to the caves to cure them while they hibernate, right? Dark, miserable places. Alouette won't want to go, and I'm not inclined to either."

"It's fine. I'll take you."

"Really?"

This did make Abeke grimace. In the past, she'd hated whenever Rend healed her. Most understood the discomfort to be necessary to healing, but Abeke had still never accepted it. The girl, however, didn't change her answer. "I do hate being your host. But I'd also hate to let the bats die like that."

"These flying mammals, why do you like them?" said Rend, "It's not my business to ask, but wasn't there a part you mentioned about threatening to murder your friend for lunch?"

"Okay, that is true. But they're nice enough, and didn't want to hurt me. Maybe I could be friends with a bat too, if I want."

"Huh. Lun, hold your arm near her," Rend instructed.

Confused but accepting, Lun did so. His arm split into red and metal limbs that extended across Abeke's clothes lightly, searching for something. Rend found it, and retracted.

"What..." said Lun, in response to that.

"Just needed to see if there were traces of that fuzz the bats mentioned. Turns out they carried it out of the cave, spread it to Abeke. Luckily, it only hurts bats. I recognize it, it's Pseudogymnoascus destructans. Fixable. Alright Abeke, I accept. Your bat buddies will be saved."

"Thank you, Rend, it means a lot." She thought of hugging Rend, but since Rend didn't quite have anything to hug, she just patted Lun's arm.

"Well," said Rend, a hint of smugness returning, "the great doctor of the forest can surely find it in him to forgive."

"Yeah. Now all that's left is to see when Bagee returns."

Beni burst through the door, and said, "Abeke! Oh, and every else. Hi. Abeke!"

"That's me."

"You'll never guess who returned!"

* * *

Everyone in the house except for Rend and Alouette rushed out of the house. They were a bit late though, as a small crowd had formed already around the demigod. Nobody quite got close to him, most standing at a distance. That included the wary Mani, the curious Tenga, and Maya.

Bagee and Maya focused on each other. The emperor couldn't tell what she thought, but backing down didn't seem wise at that point.

This continued on for a bit until Bagee broke the silence, "I'm back." For his first time home in decades, he'd imagined a better greeting. But for all he was worth, he couldn't think of anything else to say. "Hi."

"Say," Mani asked in a casual way, "did anyone ever decide what the punishment is for leaving like he did?"

Despite his hesitance, a bit of Bagee's empiric swagger returned. "You made that a crime after I left. Since I did it before the criminalization, I'm in the clear. Ex post facto. Plus, the Island's opening up again. It'd be odd to punish me for something you just made legal." He glanced at the woman who had been his mother. "You can accuse me of a lot, but not of being a criminal."

"Nice to meet you..." Tenga gave a grin. "Which name do we

use—"

"Sk- Bagee."

"Right. You know about the results of the meeting?"

"I had an informant there. Great little batty beast I know. Awesome help, and one of the few beasts perceptive enough to understand human speech. Michi will be a grand bat one day, just you wait."

Maya smiled a bit and waved, figuring she'd kept Bagee uneasy long enough. "Hi."

"Mama, I di—"

She held up a hand, and the emperor stopped. "Decades passed, during which I could've died for all you knew—"

"I had the bats keep me updated." Bagee wondered what to say. "How has it been?"

"So and so. I adopted Rollan and Abeke. And before you think so, no. They were not a replacement for you. In fact, most of the time, they're better behaved."

The emperor's heart hardened. "What, are you going to punish me? Ground me in my room?"

"No. Just tell me," said Maya, "Do you regret leaving?"

Though his eyes heated, he still said, "No."

"Fine. Well, you did leave suddenly. Couldn't contain yourself, huh? Weren't satisfied with life here."

"Yes. But," with tears in his eyes at this point, he almost stuttered, "I am sorry for not saying good-bye. I'm sorry. Please." He opened his arms, and his mama stepped into them. The onlookers either looked away in embarrassment or stepped forward to join in a giant mass of hugs that soon brought down the demigod.

"Welcome back."

* * *

Some time later, Taran and Lunate joined Bagee at the balcony overlooking the village. People milled about, as they did, though a few glanced up at the returned Islander. Bagee kneeled on the floor, his chin on the railing. He seemed tired, Taran thought. But his eyes also showed a weary satisfaction at being back.

Taran stood and leaned against the rail with his elbows, maintaining the quiet onlook over the area. Lun had his back straight, hands folded behind him in respect for the ruler of his country. This formality was perhaps a bit silly, considering how relaxed the other two were. But habits died hard.

"It's a pleasure to meet you." said Taran.

"Likewise."

"I've heard a lot about you."

"I imagine. Was any of it true?"

"Perhaps not," said Taran. "Though the person I ended up meeting is much more interesting than an aloof demigod."

Lun kept still, but Taran glanced at him before continuing, "What did you want to talk about?"

"Oh, this and that." Bagee stood up, setting his hands on the icy rail, before brushing at his outfit. "Lunate. You were the first Astrian in history to set foot on the Island. You've done a lot. We accomplished what once seemed impossible."

"Thank you." Lun said.

"I have to ask, why hasn't anyone else arrived here? I had Didae summon me to the Island before a message from Ulna could update me on the expedition."

"Captain Radial started an altercation with a stormer. The

165

Saint Carpal—"

"I hear it's definitely sunk. Ah well. Such things happen," Bagee said. From his expression, Taran imagined him trying to tally how much building the *Saint Carpal* had cost. Quite a bit, he imagined.

"We could have avoided that," Lun said, "If you'd revealed your true identity earlier and warned us of dangers like that. Will you reveal who you really are when we get back?"

"Maybe. Maybe not. Actually, I should. Astria deserves honesty."

Taran did not understand all the ways this could affect the country, but he nodded in approval.

"You know," said Lun, "I thought on what you said. About letting me decide if you were blessed or not. And, well, you wouldn't be the first ruler to declare themselves blessed under heaven. And your regime did donate plenty to temples. The worship masses you oversee are quite extravagant. If you're a devout worshiper, then all is probably forgiven."

"To be fair," said Bagee, "I do believe in them."

"And the chimera?" prodded Taran.

"That too. A bit odd to follow two faiths, but I'm an odd guy. Back during my rise to power, Ulna recommended claiming divinity as a sound morale boost. Unfortunately, Noche and Dia have never spoken to me. Maybe they're annoyed, but I take it as a good sign that a sunbeam hasn't burned me to ash."

"Getting to the point, is that what you wanted to talk about?" prompted Taran.

Bagee took a deep breath, then let it out. "No. But it's good to make small talk. Lunate, you can leave us now."

Lun almost did. But hesitating, he stopped and said, "Skap—"

"Call me Bagee here."

"Okay. Bagee, why didn't you reveal your identity in Astria, and tell us anything about the Island?"

Bagee turned away, leaning against the rail. "Maybe I should have spoken up. But I found a nice place in the world. One of the most powerful people alive, and in my mind I kept a untouched paradise as my home. The Island opening, returning to confront my mistakes... change is scary. Ironic, I know, since I incited so much change when I overthrew someone. But that's how it is. Change is scary."

Lun nodded, and walked away.

Taran decided to go slow, and said, "Michi seems quite sharp. I haven't met a beast before that could perfectly understand other species."

"Yeah. Michi translated the entire meeting for me. He'd make quite the spy, if he decided. Your plan about agents to spread knowledge across the world and empower other nations... it's very antithetical to nation-building."

Taran knew the answer to the question he was about to ask, but still asked it anyway, "Why is that?"

"The point of leading is to empower one's own people. That usually involves plundering or conquering others to build stuff in one's own land. Each out for their own, after all. Raising other lands is... unusual."

"As unusual as an odd traveler becoming an emperor?"

"Point taken."

"Seems to me you need to learn what diplomacy means."

"You just say that because you're ignorant."

"Really?" said Taran. "Upstart, I'm older than you."

"Okay, that's true. But you haven't been to the political world I live in. Every banquet and royal family is connected in some way on that continent, and if any of them got the chance, they'd backstab each other."

"So you think my plan is dumb? That Astria and the Island becoming superpowers is what'll bring world peace?"

"Well, it is true several interested people in Astria would love the plundering and conquering far off lands. But here we have different beliefs. I believe it'd be better for far-off lands to fall under Astria's control. You believe it'd be better to help them. Whose view do we trust more?"

"Well," Taran drummed his fingers on the rail, "When you say it's better to conquer and trust ourselves, I can't help but wonder if an empire stepped up to the Island and wanted to conquer it, what would you do? Let's be honest, an ambitious nation isn't going to take no for an answer unless it became a law."

Bagee didn't answer.

"Look, people from different groups across the Ring aren't on the search all the time for how to backstab each other. Most people are okay with mutual aid and help. Being friends. From what I've seen of Islanders and Astrians, I'd say it's the same all over the world. Can you believe in that?"

"Maybe. And if we raised other countries, and passed laws to avoid exploitation, perhaps we wouldn't conquer. But even with your view of the world, you have to admit not every faction in the world will be as nice as you."

"True." Taran smiled. "But I have a feeling that whoever is chosen to be these envoys, they'll do good. They'll succeed."

The two gazed down at the village for the moment, lost in imaginings of the future.

After a few moments, Bagee spoke up, "That ice pillar Rollan made is incredible. I should praise him for that."

"You're not his leader, you know."

"Right, I knew that."

"Of course."

"Hm." said Bagee. "Where did that game down there come from?"

"High-kick? The Ring."

"Really? Huh. Say, so with these envoys we're sending out, who should we choose to do it? After the laws for that are all written of course, who can be trusted for dangerous trips into obscure lands?"

Taran did not feel the need to answer. The solution was right there in front of them.

18

For The World, For The Future

In an icy tower in the tundras, on the first floor, in the middle of the city of the Skulks, Taran wrote. With colorful pigments and a feather given to him by a blue-clawed bird, Taran wrote vivid vibrant letters to people the world over and read them too. A shelf in the corner held stone-cut figures and statues.

The Chief was back home in the Ring, and ten years had passed.

Vitulina had tried to convince Taran to make his study on the highest floor of the tower. He'd laughed off the offer. Taran's knees shook sometimes and his ears skipped a sound often, so why not have an easy time walking to the first floor? Besides, Taran didn't need a high vantage point anymore, to try and stare north at the Island. He had been there and back.

A girl, dark skinned and with the same heavy clothes as Taran, although with braided hair, entered the front door. "Grandpa?"

Taran put the finishing strokes on his letter to Bagee and sealed it with wax. "Did you come to tell me the envoys returned?"

Phoca gave a toothy smile, one of her baby teeth had fallen

out. "How did you know? They just got here!"

"A guess. Take me there." Taran's necklaces, the folded hands and canine tooth, were both a little more worn these days. Both jangled as Tarn let himself be led by the hand by Phoca to the port.

The town had grown so much through international trade, clever politics, investment, and crossroads. Nobody could even call it a town anymore. Towers and bridges and buildings and temples had all been made of ice. Such a wild fusion of places, from the regal columns brought by Astria, to the tradition Skulk traditions of domes and icy bestial carvings. Nowhere near as tall as the forests of the Island, yet. But a good rival. Leather and paint and metal and wood had been injected into the skeleton of the place, decorating and binding. The Skulks had never before had such wealth and influence. Indeed, in every obvious and desirable way, the place had grown and improved.

Still, it sometimes saddened Taran as he walked the streets with his proud granddaughter. When Phoca grew up, Taran knew, she would not even remember the small homes of her infancy. Vitulina chuckled at Taran's feelings, reminding him that their culture would survive and that their descendants would enjoy prosperity, even though much of the city's population had come from abroad, to refill those deceased by the pox. The old man agreed. He still felt sad all the same.

As Phoca had said, the envoys had arrived in port. Taran also spotted a thin green vessel from Guttio and a purple regal ship from Minis. Other countries, after some bartering, had been allowed to sail north as well. From the ship of the envoys, sailors walked offboard from the gangplank. Taran headed to two of them, Lun and Abeke. Both rushed to hug and greet him. Lun had not changed much over the years. He still dressed well

171

and kept his blonde hair short. Though perhaps he rushed into things less often and almost never carried a weapon nowadays. The biggest differences were two medals he wore. One blood-red and steel-grey, showing Rend. The other dark blue and windy green, depicting Ele. Abeke had one more medal too, of a brown and grey bat, Michi.

"Old friend," said Lun, with a hand of Taran's shoulder. "How have you been?"

"Minus the hearing loss and shaky steps? Awesome. In the prime of my life." At a questioning glance from Lun, Taran clarified, "I mean it. I have a lot to be thankful for."

"Want me to examine you with Rend's help?"

Taran brushed off the hand. "Leave that for later, let's catch up. Phoca, would you give Abeke a tour around the new spots in town?"

"You mean the city?" his granddaughter asked. "Okay."

"Thank you. Abeke, we'll catch up later."

As the groups separated, Abeke said, "Incredible. We haven't seen each other in a few years and he left."

Phoca nodded like an old sage, and said, "He's busy a lot. Want to go eat something?"

"After the seasickness leaves. But show me around. Oh, hey, want to give your granddad a gift?" Seeing the girl eager, Abeke handed her a stone statue of a mantis. Phoca was eager to give it over later.

* * *

Taran and Lun strolled the bustling port streets, lined with stalls and hardy sailors. The two headed north, near the bay's mouth. Taran said, "How are Rollan and Ulna?"

"Good, still back on the ship. They might be in a relationship now, I think. Never mind all that though. You want to know how our trip south went. Some pirates attacked."

"Not a problem, I take it?"

"Not at all." Lun chuckled at remembering it. "We took them onboard as captives and left them to a local jail, but I still think Rollan went overboard. He left their ship crucified on a floating iceberg. It's stunts like that making us world-famous. After that, we found the desert people we'd meant to visit. Turns out a civil war had erupted there, between king Idrissa and his son, the prince Buchra."

"What a shame." said Taran. The two had reached the seaside, where small battlements ran along the coast. One could climb the stairs to walk along the battlements. The duo rose the stairs and leaned against the rails up top. Lun looked north, across the ocean toward the Island, while Taran gazed south at the city. Taran asked, "Which side was in the right?"

"Both, kind of. The entire conflict ended up being because the prince, Buchra, had not received enough love from his father as a child."

Even after all his time working in politics, Taran still couldn't shake the feeling things got silly sometimes. "Which side did you choose to share knowledge and technology with?"

"Both. Somehow, we managed to end the civil war by having the two meet up and punch their problems away. They'll be fine, I think. And the place surprised me. They waged war through these incredible boulder catapults and sandy mobile mountain fortresses."

Taran nodded and relaxed. "All is well that ends well." The

Chief noticed the apprehension on his friend's face. "Out with it Lunate. What troubles you?"

"Perceptive as always. Taran, I accepted your suggestion to be an envoy because it fit my role as a crusader. Exploring and learning and hacking through things, it made sense. But this mission faces challenges, considering your lofty goals. So many countries across the world are reaching out to us, begging for the envoys to visit them, to receive international aid. Some have good intentions, I think. But others definitely don't. It's a matter of time before our help goes to a despot, a ruthless ruler. What then?"

"Then we deal with it as we go. Are those doubts anything for an explorer to hold? A minor setback, then give up. A future problem, time to end it early. Did you turn back from going to the Island just because your ship sank? Of course not. Who knows, perhaps I'll even set sail again soon myself."

"At your age?"

"Why not? The world is a beautiful place. I believe she deserves every effort we can give to her. Do you agree?"

About the Author

Diligent student, amateur pianist, passionate writer, dog walker; Giancarlo Diago Cevallos is all these and more. When not satisfying his sweet tooth or biking to the library, can often be found gazing at the stars under the Miami sky.

If you want to reach out to me;
  Email address; giankid007@gmail.com
  Twitter account; @GiancarloDCE

Printed in the USA
CPSIA information can be obtained
at www.ICGtesting.com
JSHW010139050923
47750JS00022B/306